TEMPEST OVER SCOTLAND

THE STORY OF
JOHN KNOX

by
NORMAN E. NYGAARD
Author of
Deep Forest, They Sought a Country
etc.

ZONDERVAN PUBLISHING HOUSE
GRAND RAPIDS, MICHIGAN

This printing — 1963

To My Son
PHILIP MACLEAN NYGAARD
Soldier, Engineer,
Student for the Ministry

INTRODUCTION

Near the end of June, 1547, a French fleet appeared off the east coast of Scotland at the gates of the castle of St. Andrews to lay siege to this ancient university town which had become the center of the Reformation movement in Scotland.

Mary of Lorraine, widow of James V, was serving as regent in the place of her daughter, Mary "Queen of Scots," who was only five years of age at the time. Recognizing the menace of St. Andrews, not only to her own incumbency but to the potential and subsequent reign of her daughter, she had undoubtedly called for the aid of the French who had their eyes on Scotland as territory which might be added to the French crown. Mary had been sent to France to prepare her for the role of queen in view of the fact that, almost from the moment of her birth, she had been affianced to the dauphin who was later to be crowned Francis II.

St. Andrews was the seat of a great university. The preacher in the parish church that year was John Knox. Earlier he had shared the preaching responsibility with other learned men on the university faculty, but his sermons had been so challenging and he had acquired a reputation for such eloquence that he had become the regular preacher in the church and acknowledged leader of the Reformation which was sweeping Scotland at the time.

For one month the garrison at the castle stood off the attack, both by sea and by land, but on the last day of July the garrison capitulated. Aid had been promised the besieged by England and had been daily expected but it was never sent and the beleaguered Scots were overwhelmed by sheer force of numbers.

The French commander promised that if the Scots surrendered they would be transported to France and from there they could go to any country which they might choose, except Scotland. But the terms of the surrender were violated and all who were taken prisoner were detained. Some of the captives were incarcerated in dungeons in castles at Brest, Rouen, Cherbourg, and Mont St. Michel.

INTRODUCTION

Those who were regarded as the most dangerous prisoners, Knox among them, were sent to the galleys. For them the winter was spent in the harbor at Nantes. Knox was chained for the entire period. With the coming of spring the galleys were put to use, mostly as cargo vessels, transporting war *matériel* and other government stores from one port to another. Early in the spring of 1548 the galley on which Knox was imprisoned set out for duty in the Mediterranean.

1

The scent of unwashed humanity was almost more than John Knox could bear. For nine months he had been a prisoner in the French galley to which he had been consigned after the capitulation of St. Andrews, but he could never accustom himself to the smells below decks.

However, the agony of protesting muscles almost caused him to forget the pungent odors as John, one of three who were chained to the fourth bank of oars in the prison galley, pulled on the long sweep.

"About time for our relief to come, *nicht wahr?*" Friedrick Loefler, who was on John's right, remarked under his breath to the Scotsman.

"Close your mouths, vermin, criminals," shouted Jules Ferrier, the overseer, as he cracked his whip across their backs.

The whip stung, as always, but Knox had become inured to physical hurt. Still, from long custom, he winced.

Although physical coercion no longer had much effect upon him the accompanying spiritual coercion did. In his heart John resented the brutality, the coarse oaths, the contempt of his jailers. Being a stubborn Scot he could not accept his lot with resignation although he had adapted himself to it.

Loefler murmured under his breath, "Were we foreordained to this, Brother John?"

"We were," Knox replied sturdily but stealthily, "from the very beginning of time."

"But to what end?" inquired Loefler.

"The purpose is known to God. It is in His hands."

His reply was confidently uttered but John himself was puzzled. How did it come about that one who sought to do the will of God was thus persecuted? Then came reassurance to his mind. Paul had been imprisoned and burned at the stake in Rome. Even Christ had suffered imprisonment and an ignominious death on a cross.

"I prefer the theology of Brother Martin that man is justified by faith — not by works," he whispered.

"I can accept that," Knox agreed, "but I also must believe the other, for the great apostle set it forth plainly in his letter to the Roman church."

"But, as Brother Martin explains, each one of us may interpret the words of the great apostle according to the leadings of our own hearts," Loefler countered.

"Ssssh!" Knox hissed. "The overseer!"

Loefler bent his back to the oar with increased vigor.

Loefler, like Knox, was regarded as a political prisoner. He had been caught up in a widespread drive to rid the country of Protestants who had come to France to study the movement which centered in John Calvin.

Many scholars, like Loefler, traveled between Marburg, Germany, where Luther was preaching, to Geneva, where Calvin held forth, and to Zurich where Huldreich Zwingli had settled with his disciples. But many of them also came to Paris, for here the followers of the three movements rubbed elbows with one another.

Knox was a disciple of Calvin, Loefler of Luther. The Protestant movement was in a state of flux. There had been no intention on the part of its leaders to set up a Protestant church. Rather had Luther, Calvin and Zwingli sought to reform the church from within. When they finally came to the conclusion that this was impossible each had left the church reluctantly and around each of the three had crystallized what would eventually be the nuclei for separate churches.

But at the moment the followers of each were only loosely united into bands of disciples who studied the Bible and the nature of the church under their chosen leaders. And many drifted from Marburg to Zurich, to Geneva and Paris.

Luther had been a priest in the Roman Church but Calvin had never been ordained. Instead, his training had been in the field of canonical law and he had already begun to set up in Geneva a form of government which would be based upon the teachings of Scripture as he interpreted them, a government which would be both civil and ecclesiastical in character.

Luther had in mind no particular form of government for the church. It was not until some years had passed that a church was built upon the foundation of his theology. But Calvin was greatly interested in government, both ecclesiastical and temporal, and the relationship which the church sustained to the monarch. He believed that changes could be wrought which would reform the church from the top.

Followers of Luther clung to the doctrine of justification by faith and the right of the individual Christian privately to interpret the Scriptures according to the light of his own conscience. The sale of indulgences by Rome had prompted Luther's proclamation of the stirring dictum that men were not justified by good works but by faith in Jesus Christ.

Jules Ferrier walked up and down the runway which separated the two banks of oars of the prisoners. He seemed to have eyes in the back and on either side of his head, for whenever a prisoner eased up he flung a word at him and brought his whip across the man's back.

The galley was a freighter which usually plied the Mediterranean coast but occasionally called at ports in the Atlantic as well. Most of the prisoners were political but in the group there was a sprinkling of convicts who had been imprisoned for theft and other crimes. Since theft was a capital offense and merited death the number of these was limited to those whose crimes had been minor. Major crimes were punished by beheading.

But the possibility of service on a galley for opposing either the church or state served to keep politically-minded individuals in line, save for the stubborn adherents of the idea that a reformation was sorely needed in the church. Thus, among those who were pulling oars were not only excommunicated priests like Knox and Loefler but priests who had remained within the church, seeking thereby to change the mores and practices of the church from the inside.

Occasionally the political prisoners had long conversations below decks but usually they were so worn out that they dropped to the straw pallets to which they were assigned as soon as their relief came, wearied at the unaccustomed exertion of pulling on the oars to which they were chained.

Relief finally came for Loefler and Knox. Their shackles were unlocked and they were replaced by others and they marched below to fling themselves down on the pallets which had just been vacated by the other shift.

" 'Twould be a blessing if we only replaced one occupant," Knox murmured to Loefler, "but these beds are so full of other inhabitants and they are so eager to feast on our emaciated bodies that they don't give us time to get bedded down before they go to work."

"That is also foreordained?" Loefler inquired.

Knox gave a wry smile.

"I have often wondered about that," he admitted. "But you will have to agree that they have discovered a remarkable way to assist us in mortifying the flesh."

"Aye, that I will concede," Loefler replied.

A short while later buckets of food were distributed to the gang which came off duty and the rowers gathered about them. Mutton and soggy bread, with a cup of sour wine, were the ingredients of the meal. They all dipped their hands into the same bucket for the morsels which they desired.

"Like animals they feed us," murmured Loefler.

"And so they regard us," exclaimed a priest in Franciscan garb, a Frenchman named Anselm. "And so we are, to be sure, in one part of our being."

Nor had the group around the bucket out of which John Knox took his repast succumbed to the animal manner of eating which John observed in those who had been sentenced to the galleys by reason of having committed capital crimes. Although fed like animals John Knox's friends managed to eat like gentlemen. They deferred to one another, Protestant and Catholic alike, and shared their repast with consideration for the needs of all.

John was particularly concerned for the welfare of an emaciated parish priest on whose fragile body the welts of the whips stood out like ridges. The man was racked with coughing and Knox had the feeling that he would not be long for this world.

"Are you any better today?" he inquired of the priest. "Maybe I had better speak to one of the overseers and seek to have you relieved from duty for a few days."

"It would do no good," Father Paulus replied, "and 'twould only bring their wrath down upon your head."

"But it is a Protestant head," Knox suggested with a wry smile.

"In a sense we are all Protestants, Brother John," Father Paulus said gently. "I am protesting against what I have felt were iniquities from within the church. You have made your protest outside of it. But we are all children of the same God and we all love the Lord Jesus Christ and seek to keep His Church pure and unspotted from the world."

"You are a true Christian, Brother Paulus," John remarked, "for you seem to love even heretics."

"No one who loves God is a heretic, John," Brother Paulus replied. "The only heretics are those who deny Him."

John helped him to his pallet and then he, too, found his place and soon was asleep. He dreamed of the moors, the lakes and the green-clad hillsides of Scotland, of his boyhood home at Haddington. But his sleep was troubled, partly because of the vermin which crawled out of the straw to fasten themselves to his body, and partly because he was still not inured to the life of a galley slave. His flesh still protested against the treatment which it had to sustain. He seemed barely to have touched his head to the pallet when he was rudely awakened again.

"Get up off your soft beds," Jules Ferrier shouted. "Did you think you could sleep all day? Back to your shackles, you scum. Back to the smooth oars for you."

Wearily the shift arose, stretched to take the kinks out of sore muscles, and lined up in the center of the hold. Father Paulus dragged himself to his place in the line. Knox yearned to give him a hand but he knew that if he did Ferrier's whip would dig into Paulus' frail body and he would be no help to him at all.

Wearily they trudged to their task. It seemed an endless treadmill. John wondered at times how he managed to remain alive. Men died around him. When they did their bodies were unshackled and pitched overboard to become the provender of sharks and gulls.

Knox did not fear death but he had early decided that, if at all possible, he would remain alive. He had a mission to accomplish and, unless the Lord terminated that mission, he resolved to carry on.

Whips cracked over his head. The sting of the enlarged tips of the leather snakes of which the whips were fashioned bit into his back, his forehead, his neck, like huge gnats. But he did not intend to die. He would live to accomplish the purpose which God had for him.

"These overseers are all sadists," Loefler whispered to him on one occasion.

"Made in the image of God, nevertheless," John replied.

"I suppose that the Almighty had some purpose in mind," Loefler conceded.

"Watch out!" John replied with a wry smile. "You will become a convert to the teachings of Calvin."

Their cargo at the time was a load of wine casks which they had picked up in Cette for delivery to Toulon. The huge casks were distributed between decks and in the holds, and some were lashed to the main deck as well.

From Toulon they would go to Spain and then back to Marseilles. It was an interminable round, sometimes as far east as the Holy Land but rarely through the Pillars of Hercules into the Atlantic.

It was at sea on a voyage to North Africa that a conflict broke out between certain convicts. A burly farmer from the Midi began the fight and eventually all of the men below decks were involved, except those who were aboard because of their religious convictions.

The latter huddled together at one side of the hold and let the fight go on around them. Knox had no idea concerning that which had provoked the fracas, whether it was a word, a gesture or some overt act. All of the convicts were supposed to have been searched before coming aboard for any lethal weapons which they might possess, but before long knives, which had been secreted aboard, were brought into play. Blood flowed freely.

John Knox plunged into the fray to try to separate the participants but to no avail. No one paid any attention to him. He could speak French but it was the language of the scholar and not of the street, and either they did not understand him or they would pay him no heed.

"Quit it!" he shouted. "Leave off! This will only bring more punishment upon all of us. We're in this together. We should not fight one another. It but makes it more difficult for all of us when we do. Leave off, I say."

But he might as well have commanded a storm to cease.

Soon, however, overseers appeared below decks, this time wielding clubs instead of whips. Within moments the uprising was quelled. Three bodies were pulled out of the melee, dragged up the ship's ladder and tossed overboard.

One of the overseers made an attempt to ascertain who was responsible for the melee but the only explanation which he could secure from the participants was that those who were killed were fighting among themselves and that the others had only sought to separate them.

Knox discovered that his efforts at pacification had resulted in additional bruises to his face and head.

When he retired from the fray with the arrival of the over-seers Loefler remarked, shaking his head sadly, "It is preferable to let them fight. I, too, sought to separate fighters before you joined us, a fight as bloody as this battle, and learned that it was better to let them get the anger out of their systems. Always remember, John, that there are two kinds of men down in this hold, those who have committed real crimes and will always be criminals and others, like ourselves, who are imprisoned for conscience' sake. The men of ill will are forever at one another's throats. It would be difficult to change their natures. Well nigh impossible, in truth."

Yet, by reason of his interference in their quarrel, the con-victs felt a kinship for Knox. They sensed a boldness in his na-ture which appealed to them although they had scant interest in his beliefs or in his teachings. Because of this they consulted with him from time to time.

One among them, a huge blacksmith from Belfort, a man who called himself Jean DeFore, came to him often. His was a capital crime for, with his huge sledge hammer, he had crushed the head of a man who had questioned his charges for shoeing his horse.

"The man came at me with his sword," he explained simply. "True, I killed him, but it was not murder."

John Knox agreed.

"It was wrong," he said. "Yet you were but defending your-self."

"But the judges would not listen to my plea," said the smith. "In a matter of minutes they gave me a life sentence to the gal-leys. Since they knew that I could pull an oar right heartily they assigned me to this living death instead of to the headsman."

A friendship developed between the two. Knox recognized the fact that the fellow was hot-tempered and ready to fight whenever the occasion arose and he fancied himself injured by the jibes of his fellow convicts, but Knox also regarded the smith as a man who had decent human impulses and as such was wor-thy of the friendship of like-minded individuals.

DeFore took him aside one day immediately after his crew had been brought down into the hold, following their stint at the oars.

"We are due to go to Naples on our next voyage," he said. "I heard the overseers discussing it. While we are at the docks unloading some of us intend to make a break for freedom. They will not anticipate this from us since it will be difficult for us, after we have won through to freedom, to escape detection in the countryside, but we have friends there who will give us refuge until the ship sails again. Then we can make our way back to France once more."

John made no comment.

DeFore continued, "We do not intend that all shall know of our plan for someone among them might betray us to the overseers, but we would be glad to have you join us and recruit some of the religious as well."

"That I could not do," said Knox. "I am not happy in my imprisonment, to be sure, but I would not be willing to take the law into my own hands. Paul enjoins all men to be in obedience to civil authorities. These men are set over us in government and, as such, we must obey them."

DeFore shrugged his shoulders.

"We had hoped that you might join us," he said. "Some of us had counted strongly that you would. But you will not betray us?"

"Assuredly not. Each man must do what is right in the light of his own conscience. For conscience' sake I cannot join with you in the conspiracy. But by the same token I could not betray you to our captors. Such an act would be altogether abhorrent to me."

"But you wish us well?"

"Assuredly," Knox replied, taking DeFore's hand and shaking it heartily. "May God's purposes be accomplished through you. That is my prayer for you and your comrades."

"Thank you, my friend," replied DeFore.

Even though he would have no part in their conspiracy John was acutely conscious of the fact that it was being carried on around him. He could sense it in the furtive whispers of the convict group, in the significant glances which they cast at one another and at him.

The Mediterranean was calm as they made their way to Naples. The spring winds had blown themselves out and rowing, therefore, was much easier than it had been earlier in the season.

They made port at night and tied up at the wharf. On occasion they had unloaded their craft after a late arrival but this time they kept all of the prisoners below deck. It was exceedingly hot and humid in the hold and, since all the oarsmen were

confined in the one large area, there was scarcely room to
turn around, so closely were they packed together, two men
sharing a pallet made for only one.

There was little sleep that night. Men conferred in low tones
but John's comrades sought to woo sleep. He tossed restlessly,
disturbed by his knowledge of what would happen on the
morrow.

At the first light of day the buckets of food were brought below and the overseers shouted at the men, bidding them bestir
themselves and eat. Their fare that morning consisted of old
crusts of bread and cold meat.

"Eat heartily, scum," Jules Ferrier shouted. "Today we unload
our cargo and you weaklings must be well fortified for the task.
If a man drops at his work we toss him overboard. So eat your
fill."

The convicts glared at their tormentor but accepted his invitation to eat. The political prisoners stoically joined them in
the repast but showed no signs of resentment for his jibes.

Barely enough time was allotted them to bolt their food when
they were ordered to line up. The overseers were augmented by
several squads of soldiers and the convicts were herded to the
upper deck. They began at once to unload the holds, passing
huge sacks of grain from one to the other.

Apparently by chance but actually by shrewd arrangement
on the part of DeFore, John and his companions found themselves in the hold, lifting huge sacks of grain and passing them
to the men above. These latter carried them out onto the dock.

All morning long the unloading was carried on without a
hitch. The men worked without grumbling. At noon they paused
for their meager repast.

It was just after the noon meal that the signal was given and
one group of the men rushed the overseers. The others jumped
to the dock and attacked the soldiers. The surprise was so in-
stantaneous that the overseers were quickly overwhelmed.

But the soldiers on the dock had a moment to prepare for the
attack before the men came at them. They drew their swords
and laid about them. The primitive weapons which the men
had fashioned on shipboard were no match for the sharp blades
of the military.

Knox and his friends took no part in the fray but stood help-
lessly by. The discipline of the priests had been such that they
could not participate without orders from a superior, and Knox

and the reformer group believed so sturdily that obedience was due to civil authorities that they would have no part in an uprising against representatives of the crown.

On board the galley the prisoners were winning but those who had attempted to fight the guard on the wharf found themselves facing a superior and better-armed force. The soldiers laid about them with their swords, hacking to pieces those who thrust themselves upon them.

John's eyes were on DeFore. The man seemed to be winning through. He had a pike in his hand which he had wrested from one of the guards and literally mowed his way through the front rank of the military. But it was one man against an entire company of soldiers and when he burst through to the second file he was met by flashing swords which cut him down.

Knox saw DeFore sink slowly to his knees. Horror-stricken, Knox turned his head away as one soldier plunged his sword into DeFore's chest and the big man fell face forward. Soon the entire group of prisoners was beaten. Some of the men dropped to their knees to plead for mercy but their pleas were in vain. The guards used swords and pikes with telling effect upon those who were on their feet, and upon those who were dead or dying as well. The slaughter was complete.

The soldiers now converged upon the galley, mounted the gangplank, and came aboard. With the same ruthless efficiency with which they had dispatched the dockside prisoners they hewed away at the men on board ship. They stopped only when they came to the group of priests and Reformationists.

They seemed uncertain what to do at this juncture. From their habits they could see that these prisoners were either priests. or scholars. Even though they were a part of the group which had revolted, long custom decreed that they could not touch the person of a priest with a weapon and so their swords came down.

The group eyed them unflinchingly, calmly. They hesitated before them. Finally their dilemma was resolved when the captain appeared on the foredeck.

"Leave these men be," he shouted. "They are renegade priests and disobedient friars. Some of them are even Reformationists but they had no part in this uprising. Leave them be."

To the mate who stood by his side he muttered, "Besides, we need someone to man the oars."

The soldiers wiped their blades and put them back in their scabbards.

The captain then ordered the remaining prisoners to dispose of the dead. Almost immediately the priests among them began to administer the final rites of their church both to the dead and the dying.

Knox was among those who set about dragging the dead to the side of the wharf where they were unceremoniously pitched into the sea. He could not bring himself to lay a hand upon a grievously wounded man and thus dispose of him. Nor would he drag a body to the rail of the ship or the edge of the wharf without the final rite of the church to which the man belonged.

Not that he believed in the rite any longer but if those men had died in the faith which he himself had renounced they were still entitled to the ministry of that faith.

On the dock he made his way to Jean DeFore. The giant smith looked up to him through eyes which were fast glazing but which still had a spark of life in them. He had bled profusely from many wounds but the flow had stopped and he lay in a pool of congealed blood.

"I'll take you aboard," John said softly to him. "We'll bind up your wounds."

"No! No!" the smith urged. "There is no use. I'm almost gone. Besides, they wouldn't let you."

"The orders are . . ." John began.

Jean interrupted.

"I know. I heard them. Into the bay. Take me to the edge and dump me in."

"I can't," Knox protested.

"You can. You must," murmured Jean through tight-shut teeth. "I'd rather your hands . . . ."

Here his voice trailed off.

"First let me call a priest to give you absolution."

The ghost of a smile played about Jean DeFore's mouth.

"I'd rather have your prayer," he whispered.

"But I have been excommunicated."

"You are priest enough for me. Pray!"

John knelt on the rough boards of the dock and began his prayer. Unconsciously he slipped into the Latin and then stopped abruptly and prayed softly in French.

"We commit Thy servant unto Thee, O Lord," he prayed. "He has sinned grievously but repents of his sin. With Thy great

Father heart we pray that Thou wilt forgive him and wilt receive him unto Thyself. In the name of Thy Son, Jesus Christ,
our Lord, who died that all who had sinned might be reconciled
unto Thee. Amen."

"That is a good prayer, Brother John," DeFore mumbled.
"Now drop me overboard."

Gently John Knox dragged his body to the edge of the wharf,
paused for just a moment, and dropped him in. Then he turned
away to continue the grisly task. Soon all of the group had been
disposed of. Many of the bodies were still floating but most
were gradually sinking into the deep.

"All right, men," shouted the overseer. "Now get the rest
of the cargo unloaded."

When the job was finished late that afternoon the galley put
out to sea again, short-handed. Fully one-half of the oarsmen
had been killed or wounded in the fray and the rest had to pull
double as a result. But the weather was fair as they made their
way along the coast toward the Atlantic.

The good weather held as they reached the Pillars of Hercules
but then they sailed out into the choppy ocean. John's back
was a continual ache as he pulled at his oar. For two days the
voyage was exceedingly rough but finally the weather moderated
again and at last they reached their home port of Nantes where
a new group of prisoners awaited them, replacements for those
who had been killed at Naples.

2

As the new contingent of prisoners trooped on board Knox
discerned a familiar face among them. Despite the lines which
had been etched on his countenance, John recognized Sir James
Balfour who had been one of the sturdy defenders of St. Andrews when the castle was attacked the previous summer.

As he came aboard John greeted him heartily.

"I seem to recall you," Sir James remarked. "Haven't we
met before?"

"Aye," John replied. "Remember. We were together at St.
Andrews. I'm Knox."

"John Knox!" exclaimed Sir James. "But your hair is white, your back is — "

"Yes," John replied. "It's bent. 'Tis from pulling hour after hour, day after day, at the oars."

"My own back, I suppose . . ." returned Sir James tentatively.

" 'Tis not as bowed as mine," Knox replied. "Your outdoor life before we were taken prisoner had been more strenuous. The life of a scholar didn't fit me too well for this role."

"Silence, you scum, you offspring of swine," shouted Jules Ferrier, his whip seeking out their heads.

The two separated.

John's lips formed the words, "I'll see you again."

John and Sir James drew the same shift at the oars, and so later in the day, below decks, they were able to converse. Sir James had spent the first four months of his imprisonment in a dungeon at Rouen and then he had been assigned to a galley which had plied the Atlantic coast of France. Two weeks earlier the galley had ripped open its hull on a rock. Those who had been chained to the oars had gone down with the ship but the others, Sir James among them, had managed to swim ashore.

"We sought to escape," Sir James explained, "but most of us were soon captured and brought back to Rouen."

"But it is good to see you again!" Knox exclaimed.

"And I am eager to tell you, John, that your preaching in the parish church finally laid hold on my soul," Sir James told him. "I have had time to ponder your words and I am ready to confess that Jesus Christ is my only Lord and Saviour. I was numbered among the Protestants, to be sure, but mine was merely a protest against the Roman Church. Now, with you to guide my thinking, I am ready to give my life to the Reformation cause which to me is the cause of the true Church of Jesus Christ."

Tears sprang into Knox's eyes.

"Nobly said, Sir James!" he exclaimed. "If we should ever be released from this bondage you will be able to bear noble witness for Christ."

"Do not despair," Sir James remarked. "We shall one day be free. A slight shift in politics may bring us liberty sooner than you anticipate."

For several months the galley carried freight between the coastwise ports of the Atlantic, always within sight of land.

Finally, one day the vessel put out to sea, the coast of France left behind. Three days later John, peering through the oar slot, discerned land off the bow.

His heart leaped within him. Before his eyes arose the familiar outlines of the Castle of St. Andrews. His stroke faltered. There was a clash of oars.

"Dig in there, you Scotch turtle," Ferrier shouted, laying his whip on with biting emphasis. "Would you break the oars of all your fellows? Wake up!"

Knox set his eyes upon the back of the man ahead of him.

To Sir James he whispered, "I saw St. Andrews. We're off the coast of Scotland. Whither are we bound, do you suppose?"

Sir James returned in a low voice, "Since this is the port side we may be bound for London. But I did not think the French would take prisoners into English waters. There must be some new change in policy."

Later, when they retired to the hold for their meal and rest, John was in deep thought. Finally he turned to Sir James, "I saw the steeple of the place where God first opened my mouth in public to His glory; and I am fully persuaded, however weak I now appear, that I shall not depart this life, till that my tongue shall glorify His godly name in the same place."

"I am sure that you will," Sir James replied.

At the end of the rest period, as they stumbled back topside to the oars, John saw Father Paulus stumble and fall. He stepped out of line although the whips of the overseers were immediately brought into play, and knelt beside the priest. The line of marching men stopped.

Father Paulus looked up at him.

"I have finished the course," he whispered. "I have run the race. Henceforth there is laid up for me a crown . . . ."

His voice trailed off.

One of the overseers stepped over the dying man.

"He's done for," he said callously. "Over the side with him."

Father Anselm dropped out of his place in the line and came over to the dying priest. One glance at him and he began to repeat the last rites.

"Get on with it," the overseer said. "We've no time for this."

Father Anselm continued unheeding.

The man seemed about to thrust him aside but finally shrugged his shoulders.

"Well, make it short," he remarked.

Paying no attention to the overseer Father Anselm went on

with his task. He had barely finished when the death rattle in Father Paulus' throat ceased and with a gasp he expired.

When Father Anselm had made the sign of the cross over the body of Father Paulus he and Knox and Sir James Balfour between them lifted the body and, supporting it between them, carried it to the main deck. With a final word Father Anselm consigned it to the deep.

"He was a good man," Knox whispered to Sir James, "as eager that the church should be reformed as ever we have been."

"There are many such," Sir James replied.

For the remainder of the year their galley went up and down the Atlantic coast of France and never to the Mediterranean. They crossed the channel to England and Scotland occasionally but never set foot on English or Scottish soil.

In February, 1549, on a voyage to England, as they lay anchored in the Thames the captain summoned Knox and Sir James to the quarter deck.

"You are free to go," he announced.

"Free?" Knox exclaimed incredulously.

"You are John Knox, are you not?" the captain inquired.

"Aye," Knox replied.

"And you are James Balfour?" he inquired of Sir James.

"I am," Sir James agreed.

"Well, then, I have orders to release you," the captain said. "You can leave at once."

Knox had a series of notes for a book which he had been writing but Sir James had no personal belongings. The former was permitted to go below to gather up his possessions. Then they stepped off into a skiff which had come alongside and were landed some miles below London.

Their feet had barely touched the soil of England when Knox dropped to his knees.

"Let us give thanks to Almighty God for His divine providence in liberating us," Knox said. Sir James, too, knelt and joined with Knox in his prayer of gratitude for deliverance.

"How did this come about?" Sir James inquired of Knox after they rose from their knees.

"I know not," Knox replied.

Nor did either ever discover the reason for their liberation. Whether they were ransomed by friends, or the crown had intervened on their behalf, or the King of France had capriciously decided to liberate them they were never able to ascertain.

The two set off in the direction of London, stopping frequently to rest since they were unaccustomed to walking and found it difficult to drag one foot after another along the highway. Occasionally they met country people who regarded them curiously.

Finally one man stopped them to inquire who they were, from whence they came, and whither they were going.

"I am John Knox of Scotland," John replied, "and this is Sir James Balfour. We have just now been released from a French galley and we would find our way to London."

"John Knox?" the man inquired incredulously. "The reformer?"

"Aye," John replied.

"Then you must come to our house to sup," the man insisted. "I, too, am of the reformed faith and have heard of you."

Sir James and Knox exchanged quizzical glances.

"I shall be glad of a respite from walking," Knox said. "I have been chained for so long to a French oar that my legs tire easily."

"I, too," Sir James added.

It was a simple cottage to which their new-found friend took them. Set off from the road by a grove of trees, it was a house with a thatched roof. As they entered they stepped at once to the merry fire which blazed on the hearth. Their host drew up stools for them and they were seated, stretching out their feet toward the blaze.

"Wife!" the man shouted. "Come here! We have guests from abroad."

A face peered around the corner of an open doorway.

"Do not be a-feared," their host exclaimed. "These are friends of our own faith."

The woman came timidly into the room.

"We have oft heard in our meetings about John Knox of Scotland," the man remarked to his wife. "Well, this is he — just now released from imprisonment on a French galley. And t'other is Sir James Balfour, one of the defenders of St. Andrews when the French took it two years ago."

His wife curtsied to the two guests.

"I am sorry — so great was my surprise when we met — that I failed to give you my name," said their host. "I am Will Powell. This is my good wife, Sarah."

"We bid you welcome to our home," she remarked timidly.

"Indeed we do," her husband added.

"I'll prepare a meal at once," she said.

"Do not trouble yourselves," John objected. "We must go on to London."

"You'd do best to tarry a while," Will returned. "'Tis a good thirty miles, and if you do not yet have your walking legs 'twould be better to rest before you set out on such a journey."

"But we would not inconvenience you," Knox returned.

"'Tis no inconvenience," she replied.

"And we would learn of your adventures — or misadventures," added Will.

"It would be good to eat a meal like a Christian once more," suggested Sir James wistfully.

Knox shrugged his shoulders.

Sarah busied herself with preparations for the meal. She hung several pots over the fire and within moments a meal was set on the table.

The two guests drew their stools to the table.

"Ah, John, have you ever seen such a meal as this?" Sir James remarked.

Knox smiled.

"Never," he replied. "For months now," he explained to his hostess, "we have eaten the vilest food that men could prepare out of iron pots. 'Tis good to dine like Christians once more."

"Say a word of thanks for both of us, John, to the good Lord who brought us to this hospitable home," Sir James remarked.

"We had scarce time for such on shipboard," John said. "Our thanks had to be hasty or we got naught to eat."

Will and Sarah beamed at them, then closed their eyes while John said a simple prayer over the repast.

The meal finished, Sir James sighed.

"Never in my lifetime have I enjoyed such a repast," he remarked to his host and hostess. "I shall always remember it."

"Indeed," Knox added, "but now, Sir James, we must be off."

"Can you not spend a few days here?" his host inquired. "You will be able to recover from your experience and walk a little each day to ready yourselves for the journey to London."

"We would like to, friends," Knox returned, "but we should be on our way."

"Nay, nay, Brother John," Sir James objected. "Will is right. We would do better to bide a while with these good folk if they will have us."

Impatiently Knox murmured, "But we should . . ."

"And what do we know concerning London?" Sir James continued. "We know not even who is now on the throne. We do not know how the Reformation is progressing. Better to bide here and let Will tell us what has occurred during the time that we have been at the oars. Then we will know where to go and what to do when we arrive in London town."

"You are right, Sir James," Knox agreed, "but I would not be a burden to these good friends."

"Our home is yours for as long as you will stay," Will assured him.

They rested all morning but in the afternoon they set out to view the countryside. They helped Will with a few simple chores. They even tried to aid him with the milking but their fingers had never been accustomed to a cow's teats and they soon gave up.

That night they sat long in front of the cheerful fire which was burning on the hearth. As they gazed into the glowing coals Will briefed them on what had happened in England during their absence.

"King Henry is dead, you know," he said, "and a protectorate has been set up. Archbishop Cranmer is striving valiantly to keep alive the cause of the Reformation and is sending chosen preachers into all of the districts of the kingdom to acquaint people with the Protestant beliefs."

"How are they received?" asked Sir James.

"They find much opposition," Will replied, "but they have been chosen by the protector and the council and there is little that the opposition can do to thwart them since they are preaching with the approval of the council which is acting for the king."

"This would be something that you could do, John, to advance the cause of the Reformation," suggested Sir James. "We must confer with the authorities when we get to London. Whom should we see?" he inquired of Will.

"Archbishop Cranmer is the one who is choosing these preachers," Will replied. "I should see him if I were you."

"Would he be agreeable to engaging a Scot for such service?" asked John.

"He would if his name was John Knox," returned Will. "He has brought from Germany Peter Martyr, Martin Bucer, Emanuel Tremellius, and Paul Fagius to teach at Oxford and Cambridge and they have been well received."

"Then we shall see him," said Sir James decisively.

3

Knox was impatient to be on his way to London but Balfour
and his host and hostess kept urging him to stay and so it was a
week before they set out for the city. Sir James wanted the Scot to
be ruddy of cheek and strong of limb before he appeared at the
home of Cranmer, and the Powells were equally anxious to have
him fit for the journey. When they finally left Knox felt stur-
dier and stronger by far than when he had stepped off the galley.

He was still stooped from the oars, nor would he ever again
be able to walk altogether upright, but the good meals which
he enjoyed had brought the flesh back to his skeletal frame and
Sarah Powell had washed and patched his clothing until he
looked once more almost like the scholar that he was.

It was with light hearts, therefore, that the two friends made
their way cityward.

"How, think you, will we be received?" Knox inquired of
Balfour.

"From all that our hosts have told us I believe a welcome will
await us," Sir James replied. "I had always regarded his grace,
the archbishop, as something of an opportunist but he seems to
have become altogether Protestant in his beliefs and he evidently
wants England to be the same."

Nevertheless, it was with some trepidation that the two entered London, the objects of curious glances from the people
whom they met. Neither Sir James nor Knox had ever been in
the city before but they had no difficulty in locating Westminster
Abbey since its towers dominated the skyline.

He and Sir James came to the abbey and inquired of a clergyman whom they met where they might find the archbishop.

"In the chapter house hard by," the man said.

"Would it be possible to see him?" Sir James inquired.

"That I could not tell you," the man replied. "There are
scores of people daily who would have audience with him. You
might have to wait for some time."

"We have just been released from servitude aboard a French
galley," Sir James explained. "We were taken prisoners when
the castle of St. Andrews capitulated nineteen months ago."

"Ah, yes," the cleric replied. "Was not John Knox one of the prisoners? Do you have any tidings of him?"

"This is John Knox," said Balfour, indicating John with an inclination of his head, "and I am James Balfour."

"John Knox!" the clergyman exclaimed. "The fiery preacher from the parish kirk at St. Andrews?"

"The same."

"Well, then, come with me. The archbishop will want to see him at once," the cleric said. "John Knox! I can scarce believe it. You do not appear the fire-eater you are reputed to be."

Knox smiled.

"The galleys played their part in putting out some of the fire," he said.

Together the three went to the chapter house where Archbishop Cranmer lodged.

They were admitted at once and went immediately to the archbishop's chamber. Here their new-found friend explained their mission to a young cleric who excused himself immediately and went into the bishop's study.

"He will be free to see you in a moment," the young man said as he rejoined them. "He is eager to hear of your experiences and to meet both of you."

In a short time the archbishop himself opened the door and came over to greet them.

"We have heard much concerning you," he said. "Your fame has preceded you over the border. Come in that we may learn more of what befell you in the hands of the French."

They entered his chamber and he motioned to them to be seated.

The archbishop scrutinized Knox with frank curiosity.

"I know not what I had expected," he said, "but I had thought to see a towering Scot of highland dimensions. You pack considerable thunder into a small bundle."

For the first time in months Knox broke into laughter.

"I am only a simple country preacher," he replied. "I come from a humble family."

"With an eloquence that is not surpassed anywhere in Scotland or England," interposed Balfour.

"You are aware, are you not," the archbishop asked, "that it would not be wise now to return to Scotland? That unhappy country is under the thumb of France and if you were to go

back there you would be apprehended once more and returned
to the galleys."

"But that is where I must continue my ministry," Knox objected.

"To be sure," Cranmer replied, "but all in good time. It would
serve no useful purpose to be there now."

"What would you suggest?" asked Knox.

"That you preach here in England instead," replied the archbishop. "The king's privy council has given me leave to appoint
chaplains in ordinary to the king and to send these chaplains on
missions to the various districts of the kingdom to indoctrinate
both clergy and people with the purposes of the Reformation.

"You see, there are many of our clergy who continue with the
old rites and practices of Romanism. It is the plan of the council
in this manner to acquaint them with Protestant principles and
doctrines. You would preach and teach — not as the minister of
a parish but as a visiting lecturer. Your stipend would come from
the crown, as well as your authority. The stipend is not large
but it is enough to provide a living for you.

"You would have the backing of the Duke of Somerset as well
as my own support. Yet it is not an easy task which you would
undertake. There is considerable opposition to our preaching and
teaching. Coupled with that, you are a Scotsman, and the tra-
ditional enmity of our two nations would make some of our
clergy and our people hold you in suspicion. Under these circumstances do you want to undertake this assignment?"

"I would indeed be happy to do so. 'Twill give me an opportunity to try my wings again. I have not preached now for
well nigh on two years and perhaps I may have lost the gift."

The archbishop smiled.

"Think you, Sir James, that John Knox could ever lose the
ability to preach?" he inquired of Balfour.

"Sooner the sun lose its ability to shine," Sir James replied.

"Good. Then what would you think of beginning your ministry
in Berwick?" Cranmer inquired. "It is near the border of
Scotland and our people have intermingled despite the unfortunate wars between our nations. You may find many Scots
there and the people of Berwick are friendly to them. Then,
too, they will be accustomed to your speech whereas in the
south it would be almost an alien tongue."

Knox's heart leaped within him.

Berwick was on the Tweed which had its source in the land
of his birth. As he walked beside its waters he would see a

stream which had its inception in Scotland. The rain which fell on Scotland would flow by his door.

" 'Twould be wonderful to minister there," Knox agreed.

"And now, sir," said the archbishop, turning to Balfour, "what would you do?"

"I should like to return to Scotland at the earliest opportunity," Balfour replied. "If I may have leave from you and the protector to journey to the north with Knox, and then cross the border when it is safe to do so, I would appreciate it."

"I can speak for the protector," returned Cranmer, "when I say that we shall be happy to grant you leave to do so. But I would give you this word of caution. Scotland is allied with the French and you will need to exercise caution lest you fall into the hands of enemies and find yourself pulling an oar once more in a French galley."

"I would not return to St. Andrews," Balfour replied. "Instead, with your permission, I should like to go to Edinburgh and seek out friends there."

" 'Tis granted. You may be able to help our friend begin his ministry in Berwick for I am certain that you will find old friends among the good people of that city."

Knox and Balfour remained in London for a week. They listened to the discourses of the clergy and lecturers in the chapter house. John learned from them that, while officially the break with Rome had been irrevocable, many bishops and priests still carried on the rites of the church.

The first Book of Common Prayer had just been published and they read it with avid interest.

" 'Tis a popish instrument, Sir James," Knox exclaimed as they read it together. "It has no meat on its bones. The mass is still here. Christ is crucified afresh every time they celebrate it. Did they not realize that when Christ said, 'This is my body' He did not mean that He himself had entered into the wafer but that it stood for the flesh which was crucified on Calvary, and that when He said, 'This is my blood,' He did not thereby signify that He was present in the flesh but that the wine represented His precious blood once and once only shed on Calvary?"

"Yes," agreed Sir James, "and I note that only the wafer is given to communicants. The wine is still reserved to the minister."

"Yet the communion is the very heart of our faith, the Lord's Table prepared for all believers," John reminded him.

"We must see that the book is changed, man," exclaimed Sir James.

"We will," asserted Knox with conviction.

Sir James and Knox were outfitted with new clothes by their friends in London before they started for Berwick and the archbishop arranged for them to travel north in a coach which was provided by one of the members of the privy council.

"The sturdiest Protestant in all of Berwick is Elizabeth Bowes. The same cannot be said for her husband, for he is lukewarm to the cause, but Elizabeth is tireless in her labors on our behalf. I shall give you letters of introduction to her and she will greatly assist you in your labors," the archbishop explained.

Knox was in high spirits as he set out with Sir James for the north country. He would be preaching and teaching again. The fact that northern England was only partially committed to the cause of the Reformation did not deter him in the least. It merely offered him a challenge which he was not loath to accept. The journey was made by easy stages. They stopped occasionally en route, spending every night along the way with friends who had been recommended to them.

When they arrived in Berwick they went at once to the Bowes' home. Evidently the Bowes were people of some substance for their house was an exceedingly imposing edifice. Built of stone, it was evidently of considerable antiquity and it was located near the center of the city. Succeeding generations had added to the original building for it had an inner court about which the living quarters had been erected, after the fashion of a medieval castle.

They presented themselves at the gate and when the keeper had announced their arrival by sending a stableboy to the house they were warmly welcomed by Dame Elizabeth Bowes herself.

"I had never thought to meet you, John Knox," she exclaimed, "nor you, Sir James. The story of your heroic defense of St. Andrews gave us courage here in England to carry on despite the obstacles which we have met. 'Twas a sorry matter indeed that English troops failed to come to your aid in the siege. They should have been fighting shoulder to shoulder with you in defense of the town and the castle."

"True, we had expected aid from that source," Sir James remarked, "but England was struggling at the time to establish its own reformation and we had no right to expect contingents of troops to come to our aid."

"It would have united us in the common struggle," she returned drily. "As it is, Scotland is fighting for liberty from the papacy and we have not yet firmly established the cause here in England. God grant that both lands may soon be free!"

"Amen!" said Sir James and Knox in unison.

At this moment a young woman slipped into the room, pausing for a moment on the door sill. John Knox had never known romantic love. Serious-minded, apparently, from the moment of his birth, he had early given himself to the Reformation movement which became his only love and to which he gave complete devotion.

But the sight of the young woman with her piquant face, chestnut-colored hair, and deep blue eyes, stirred his pulses and made him conscious of his bent back and gnarled hands.

Dame Bowes turned.

"Marjory, dear," she remarked, "these men are John Knox and Sir James Balfour. You have heard of both. They were among the defenders of St. Andrews and have just recently been released after serving on a French galley. This is my daughter Marjory," she continued, addressing the two men.

Both of them bowed to acknowledge the introduction.

"I have indeed heard of them," Marjory said.

"John Knox is under appointment from the king to preach and teach here in Berwick, and in other cities of this area," Dame Bowes continued. "They bring letters of introduction from the archbishop."

"Mother is more of a reformer than any of the clergy in Berwick," Marjory replied with a smile which lighted up her face. "I'm not sure that father approves."

"I'm certain that he doesn't," Dame Elizabeth remarked with asperity.

She went on to explain. "Richard is not an enemy of the Reformation," she said, "but he is cautious and he does not want to antagonize those who occupy stations of importance in government and in the church. He believes that we should wait and see which party evidences the greatest prospects of winning before we declare ourselves."

"But Mother has committed herself all the way," Marjory added.

"Is your father home?" Dame Elizabeth inquired.

"No, Mother. He left some time ago," Marjory replied.

"No matter," her mother remarked.

She turned to her two guests.

"You must plan to stay with us until you can get comfortable lodgings," she said. "We would be honored to have you as our guests."

"We would not put you to such inconvenience," John Knox replied.

"It is no inconvenience," Dame Elizabeth returned, "and it will give you time to look about."

"But I must be on my way to Scotland," Sir James added. "I merely wanted to journey this far with my good friend and see him established here."

"That was most laudable," Dame Elizabeth replied, "but you had best tarry for a time. Scotland is no place now for a defender of St. Andrews. You would be arrested immediately and returned to the galleys."

"I am sure that I could find refuge with friends," Sir James suggested.

"I have no doubt but what friends would gladly shelter you," she said, "but before you could find them you would be apprehended by those who are opposed to the Reformation. No. You must not think of leaving now. Stay with us until it is safe for you to cross the border."

Knox and Balfour decided to remain but were quite surprised when they supped with the family that evening to discover that the family consisted not of the husband, wife and one daughter which they had imagined, but that the Bowes were parents of fifteen children. Four of them were married and lived in their own homes. Marjory, the fifth child, was the eldest of those who remained at home.

The family was eager to hear from Knox and Balfour the story of their adventures in the French galleys. But Richard Bowes, the father, was patently not interested. He retired to a corner of the great hall where he busied himself with documents which were apparently related to his business.

But the children gathered about Knox and Balfour, clamoring for stories of their experiences. They had to tell and re-tell these stories. When they retired for the night Sir James remarked to John, "That was more tiring than pulling an oar."

Knox added, "I have never been so worn out from my preaching as I was after giving an account of our imprisonment to those eager children."

Slyly Sir James suggested, "I noted that Marjory was most

interested in your tale. Unless I am greatly mistaken she has elected you as her hero."

"She is young and impressionable."

"But she has reached the age where she should be considering marriage," Sir James added. "How is it that you have never married, John? After Luther left the priesthood he took unto himself a wife."

Knox colored.

"I suppose that I have been wedded too strongly to our cause," he replied, "and even though I left the church I suspect that the vow of celibacy which I took prevented me from becoming interested in any woman as a wife."

"Your break with the church will be final and absolute when you do marry, John. Until then it will only be partial," Sir James said.

"Old habits of thought cling to one with strange obstinacy," Knox replied.

It was a kindly household albeit Mr. Bowes made no attempt to disguise a lack of enthusiasm for his guests and the cause to which they adhered, and Dame Elizabeth, who was an exceedingly garrulous woman, sought to confide in John doubts about her soul's salvation.

Both Sir James and Knox felt surfeited by kindness, and the noise and clamor of children finally began to wear on their nerves.

"We must find lodgings, John," Sir James remarked after they had spent a week with the Bowes. "I am constantly distracted by these dear children. They don't give me a moment's peace."

"You are right, Sir James," Knox agreed. "Today we shall seek out some quiet place where we can have time to think and where, when we pray, we shall not be interrupted constantly by the bairns."

They set out the next day to seek such a location and easily encountered one in a simple cottage, the home of an aged couple, the Edward Coppersmiths.

Despite the protests of Dame Bowes they moved into it in a few days.

"I had hoped to have you near at hand where I might converse with you often regarding the cause which is so near to our hearts," Dame Bowes objected. "And I would also like to have you close by that I might talk with you concerning my own soul's salvation."

"We are still near. The Coppersmiths live but a short distance from your gracious home," John Knox remarked. "And you are well aware of the fact that your good husband does not look with favor upon us."

Dame Bowes sighed.

"I had confidently expected that if you were to stay with us he might see the light," she replied.

"If we leave he will possibly become more interested in our cause," Knox suggested. "Now he regards us, with good reason, as intruders in his own home. You have sensed that, have you not?"

Elizabeth sighed.

"Yes, indeed," she agreed. "But he must be made to join us. He cannot remain unsaved and uninterested in the cause of freedom."

"We hope that he will," Sir James replied, "but if he does it must be of his own free will. We cannot coerce him."

Dame Elizabeth nodded her head but Knox was certain in his own mind that she was not convinced such was the way to win him.

They packed their few belongings and soon they were established in the vacant chamber of the Coppersmith home.

4

As befitted one who bore a commission from the king, albeit the monarch was too young to have affixed his personal signature to the document, Knox was invited to preach the following Sunday. The invitation came from Bishop Tonstal himself. The letters which Knox bore actually assigned him to preach for a time in the pulpit of the Berwick church so the bishop was obligated to invite him although he had little zeal for the Reformation movement. After becoming established in Berwick Knox was to preach in other churches of the district.

Never had the church been so stirred by a sermon as it was by the one which John Knox preached. He probably would not have preached with as much fervor as he exhibited had not the bishop arranged that mass would first be celebrated and the sermon would follow thereafter.

During the years of his priesthood Knox had often gone through the familiar rites of the Eucharist and knew by heart the words used in their celebration. The only difference between the mass of the Roman Church and that which was held in Berwick was that the former was in Latin while the celebrant of the mass in Berwick went through the rites in the English tongue.

The church was filled, for word had gone out that the famous John Knox would preach. People were standing in the rear and around the wall. They had expected a rousing sermon for they had heard that he was a veritable flame of fire in the pulpit, with thunder and lightning rolled up into one bundle, but they had not anticipated a discourse which would be as fiery as the one which thundered forth from the pulpit that morning.

John took for his text the familiar passage in which Jesus instituted the Holy Supper on the night of His betrayal.

"Jesus said, 'This is my body, broken for you. This do in remembrance of me . . . . This cup is the new covenant in my blood which is shed for many for the remission of sin . . . . Drink ye all of it . . . . For as often as ye do eat this bread and drink this cup ye do show forth the Lord's death 'til He come,'" slowly and softly he began.

He continued, "And on that night our Lord Jesus Christ was present among them in the flesh. Not yet had He been nailed to the tree. His disciples knew that He was there among them. They saw Him, conversed with Him at the table. He did not become a piece of bread or a cup of wine. He was there in human guise, albeit He was also the Son of God.

"And He gave both the cup and the wine to all who were present, not withholding from any one of them the two precious elements.

"But here this morning we have had a service of communion which departed altogether from our Lord's teachings. The attending priest blessed both the bread and the cup and thereby sought to change them from material elements into the actual body and blood of our Lord Jesus Christ.

"Yet the very heart of all Protestant teaching is that Jesus Christ died only once upon Calvary. Once — for all time —

He went through the agonies of the Crucifixion and the death of the Cross that believers for all time might be saved.

"Has our struggle for the truth been for naught? Are we to return to a rite which we gave up when we sought liberty from Rome? I, too, was a priest of the church. It was with reluctance that I laid aside the priestly garb that I had worn to become one with you in your search for freedom.

"There are evidently those among us who yearn for the flesh-pots of Egypt, who have given lip service to the Reformation but in their hearts are still wedded to the *paip** and to Rome."

He paused to give full effect to his words.

Then came the lightning.

"Jesus said, 'No man can serve two masters, for either he will hate the one and love the other . . . !' And I say to you that ye cannot be half in Rome and half in the Reformation. Ye cannot give lip service to the cause of freedom and yet have one foot in the church with which you have broken."

In similar vein the sermon went on. There are those who would call it ranting. Certainly John Knox was a forceful and forthright preacher, lacking tact and with no fear of offending men and women of high or low estate.

A group of people rose to leave in the middle of the peroration.

"The devil encourages you to depart," he shouted at them. "He cannot stand truth for he is the enemy of all truth. May God give you light."

The people continued on their way.

Knox condemned the nobility for their half-hearted support of the Reformation, the clergy for clinging to the ancient rites of the religion from which they had departed. His deep voice rumbled on and on. Finally his sermon came to an end.

He pronounced the benediction and the congregation left.

There was a buzz of comment as they departed.

A sturdy blacksmith remarked to a carpenter, "Mon, what a sairmon. He fairly knocked out the gentry with his thunder."

Both were Scots who had come to England to escape perse-cution.

"Aye," the carpenter replied, "and he didn't spare the priests either. The auld bishop was a-squirmin' in his chair. I'll wager he'll get off a hot epistle to the king's privy council or whatever they call it."

* pope

A carter joined them.

"Never have I heard such preachin' from that pulpit," he remarked. "The wee mon seemed to be a-blaze."

"He lived up to his repute," exclaimed the carpenter.

"Aye, they feared him in Scotland more than Beelzebub himself," said the blacksmith.

"Think you he'll preach the comin' Sabbath?" asked the carter.

"Not if the bishop can prevent him."

"Can he?"

"I know not. He is here by authority of the privy council and the Archbishop of Canterbury himself, just as that foreign mon was some time past," replied the carpenter.

"Did you ever hear a more stirring preacher?" Marjory Bowes remarked as the family drove home from the service. "It stirred me right down to my toes."

"Terrible! Terrible!" her father replied. "Rabble-rousing. The man flouted the nobles, our honorable clergy, the fine citizens of Berwick."

" 'Twas a magnificent sermon," Dame Elizabeth objected. "And it was one which was much needed here. We have been fast dropping back into our old habits of worship. And it was a mass. It was not the Eucharist of our Reformation faith."

"And what is the matter with the mass?" Richard inquired. "Just because we have broken our ties with the Roman pontiff does not mean that we should give up the hallowed practices of our faith which have come down to us from the days of our Lord."

"But as John Knox explained," returned his wife patiently, "the mass is not the Lord's Supper as He instituted it. And we must remember that He gave the cup to all of His disciples."

"They were all consecrated priests."

"No, father, they were not. They were our Lord's friends," Marjory interposed.

"Silence, daughter!" he commanded. "Would you challenge the opinions of your own father? I tell you the man is a menace. He would not only corrupt the church and our noble citizenry but he would enter into a man's own household to turn daughter and mother against the head of the house."

No more was said on their way home.

As John Knox and Sir James made their way to their lodgings Sir James remarked, "You certainly did not lose your ability to

stir men's hearts in the French galleys, John. 'Twas a magnificent sermon but I'll venture to say that you made many enemies."

"For myself I care not, as you know," John replied. "I may
have smoked out enemies of the Lord, but that is my mission.
That is what the Lord made me do."

"However, I noted some persons nod with approval," Sir
James remarked. "No doubt you also rallied those who have been
afraid to declare themselves. If they can gain courage sufficient
to stand for the right that will be a real gain for our side."

"But will they stand fast?" Knox asked. "Some of them seem
to be leaves, blown about by every wind that rises, without
purpose and without direction."

"Yes, to be sure," agreed Sir James, "but if the wind blows
strongly enough in one direction they will be joined to that
wind whether they will or not."

Although he had not been present at the service Tonstal, the
bishop of Durham, soon heard about the sermon which John
Knox had preached. He was a cultured, scholarly man but wholly
out of sympathy with the Reformation. He had been able to
hold the clergy in line with his thinking by subtly warning them
that they would lose their appointments if they sought to change
the form of worship in their churches.

As soon as he heard about Knox's preaching he summoned
him to his home. Knox and Sir James accepted the invitation
and on Wednesday repaired to the episcopal residence.

"Unfortunately, I was not on hand to greet you when you arrived in Berwick," he began, "although I had left instructions
that you should be invited to preach; for your fame, of course,
had reached me ere this and I had word from Archbishop Cranmer of your coming. He intimated that you were a forceful
preacher but we had not been prepared for a message which
was quite as strong as the one which you delivered on Sunday."

"I but spoke the words which the Lord gave me to speak,"
Knox replied simply.

"No one could doubt your sincerity," the bishop replied
mildly. "But you should know something of the temper of our
people. We are committed to the Reformation, to be sure, but
our approach to it is gradual. People cannot break off old
habits of worship for new at the rapid pace which you evidently
espouse.

"If, as the archbishop indicates, you are to preach in this

area over which I exercise jurisdiction, you will need to temper your preaching to the thinking of our people. We will welcome your aid but only if you can modify your mode of speech. Be temperate in all things, as Saint Paul urges."

Sir James smilingly interjected, "You cannot understand what you ask this man of God to do. He speaks from the conviction of a burning heart. Before he was taken prisoner by the French and forced to serve in the galleys he was like a burning torch in Scotland. I can assure you that service in a French galley to which he was consigned by reason of his activity on behalf of the Reformation did not lessen his burning zeal."

"Would you have me approve the popish mass?" asked John.

"No. Certainly not the popish mass," returned the bishop. "But we do not consider the mass the property of Rome. It is the Holy Eucharist, the sacrifice of our Lord Jesus Christ."

"But Christ is crucified afresh — or so the mass indicates — every time the mass is celebrated. And why should the laity be denied the cup and it be reserved only for the celebrants? 'Twas not thus that our Lord administered the Holy Eucharist when the table was first set in Bethany. Nor did the Early Church so celebrate the Lord's Supper. That which I preach is a return to the practice of the church in the first century."

"I see that there is no way to convince you," replied the bishop coldly. "I shall have to forbid you to preach again in the church and I shall give a full report of the sermon to the Archbishop of Canterbury."

"Do that," Knox retorted.

He and Sir James immediately departed.

"Now what shall we do?" asked Sir James.

"Perhaps Dame Elizabeth can advise us," replied John.

"Her daughter Marjory might also be of assistance," Sir James suggested blandly.

"She is over young to have an opinion in such a matter," Knox innocently replied.

Sir James' only reply was a hearty laugh.

Dame Elizabeth's indignation reached the boiling point when they told her about their conversation with Tonstal.

"I had expected as much from him," she sputtered. "He is sly as a fox. He gives lip service to the Reformation but his heart is not in it. But we can find a meeting place. Never fear."

She was as good as her word. Within a week she had persuaded the Monmouths, one of the principal families of Berwick and staunch adherents of the Reformation movement, to open their home for Sunday services and, by word of mouth, the news was published abroad that John Knox would hold forth in the great hall of their home on the following Sabbath.

Knox was even more vehement in his preaching than he had been the previous Sabbath. The hall was filled and, since it was not a church, there was a hum of conversation as the people flocked into it, a conversation which was only stilled when Knox rose to speak.

Knox began by roundly denouncing the bishop and his advisors. "A blind shepherd of sheep is he," he shouted. "And how shall the blind lead the blind? With one foot in Rome the other is only halfway in England. He is traitor to his king, to his church, and to his Lord. Our Lord said, 'Ye cannot serve God and Mammon,' but he is attempting that impossible feat."

Both Marjory and her mother were present, Marjory listening with rapt attention to the words of the preacher, her mother equally interested. Richard Bowes was conspicuous by his absence.

At the close of the service John Knox announced, "On the coming Lord's Day we shall serve communion here by the gracious leave of our host, but it shall be served in the Protestant manner. Both the bread and the cup will be given to all who come."

The very next day Bishop Tonstal dictated a letter to his amanuensis, informing the Archbishop of Canterbury of the derelictions of Knox.

> When I received your grace's letter advising me of the coming of this person I assumed that he was a scholar of note and I received him accordingly. Imagine my surprise to learn from those who attended the service in the church on the following Sunday that, far from being a savant, he actually was a former galley slave on a French vessel. Add to that, he gratuitously insulted the clergy and the leading citizens of Berwick. He criticized those who celebrated the Eucharist and he would, so he said, give the wafer to the laity as well as to the clergy, thus breaking a hallowed tradition.
>
> Naturally I have denied him the right to preach in the church, but yesterday he spoke in the home of one who has been something of a troublemaker, albeit he is a man of some considerable wealth and position. All the more pernicious is his influence, therefore. I beg of you to recall him and inform the privy council that he has stirred up our city in a most unfortunate and obnoxious way.
>
> Surely your grace would have no part in such an undertaking. Hence, this letter which I am sending by private courier,

hoping that ere another fortnight passes the man will be recalled and summarily dismissed from the service of the privy council. I am confident that my lord, the Duke of Somerset, would never countenance such preaching in the name of his majesty and the privy council.

Cranmer laughed when he received the epistle.

"It was evidently a good choice which we made when we sent Knox to Berwick," he remarked to his secretary. "He has stirred up Tonstal and evidently created a furore in the city. Do you write to Knox and inform him that we have received such a missive but that he is to disregard the bishop entirely and continue with his preaching. And send a letter to Tonstal informing him that we shall expect his wholehearted acquiescence in arranging for Knox to preach not only in Berwick but in the surrounding towns as well.

"I would that all of those who have gone forth to indoctrinate our clergy and our people were as forthright and vigorous as that Scot. England would be able to proceed more rapidly to become a Protestant nation if we had others like him."

"But is he not moving too rapidly?" inquired the secretary cautiously.

"Not at all," replied Cranmer. "King Henry has been long dead and England is still far from being the Protestant nation that Switzerland and Germany have become. And even in France there is a more solid foundation than we have here for the Reformation. If the church is to be wholly independent of Rome it must shake off the shackles of papal forms and ceremonies."

The letter which Knox received heartened him considerably. He shared it with Dame Elizabeth Bowes and the Monmouth family and, as he began his service in the great hall at the latter's home on the following Sunday, he divulged its contents to the congregation.

After a lengthy discourse in which he pointed out that the bishop and many of the clergy of Berwick were like the Hebrew tribe of whom Hosea said, "Ephraim is a cake not turned," he pointed out that the church would have to go all the way into the Protestant movement if it would have truly set its feet in the Reformation.

Knox celebrated the Lord's Supper as he had promised by giving both the bread and the cup to all who attended. Instead of the wafer to which the communicants were accustomed he used ordinary bread which the Monmouths provided.

He prepared them for this innovation, however, by reminding them that when Jesus inaugurated the supper He had used the unleavened bread which remained after they had consumed the Passover meal which preceded it. Since there were several hundred people in attendance Monmouth had provided five silver goblets for the wine and these were passed from hand to hand so that the communion service actually took much less time than the mass to which they were accustomed.

He explained his reasons for giving the cup to all communicants by saying, "Our Lord Jesus gave the cup to all who were present when this Christian feast was initiated. It was not set apart alone for the disciples but it was given to all. Among them doubtless was John Mark, nephew of the Apostle Peter, who, as we have reason to believe, was present that night, for the home in which the Supper was celebrated was probably his mother's. And others were there as well."

Knox's thundering voice was quiet now and a solemn hush descended upon the entire group. They seemed to sense the fact that they were making history.

Marjory whispered to her mother, "Do I dare take the cup? Father would not approve."

"Yes, indeed, my dear," her mother replied. "Whether or not your father approves is not important. I believe that God does and that is the important thing."

Very hesitantly, looking about them to see what others were doing, all of those present accepted the cup and took a sip, passing the goblet from hand to hand.

There was less conversation as they left the hall than there had been on the previous Sunday. People who had commented vocally before quietly went out from the service.

Only Dame Elizabeth and Marjory lingered after the service was over.

"I had but one doubt as I took the cup," Marjory confided to John Knox when he greeted her. "I did not feel worthy to drink wine which signified the Lord's blood — even though, to be sure, I knew that it was not actually such — " she hastily added. "I could see how oft I had sinned against my Saviour and I felt that it was not meet that I should drink."

"That is the way you should feel," John Knox replied. "If you had felt worthy then would you have been unworthy. The bread and wine are for those who truly repent of their sins and resolve to live a more holy and righteous life. That you did resolve, did you not?"

"Truly! Truly!" she replied.

"Then, indeed, it was right for you both to eat and to drink of the elements which represent the body and blood of our most blessed Saviour," John replied.

Dame Elizabeth was impatient, however, with anyone, aside from herself, who had problems concerned with the soul. She therefore terminated the conversation between the two by saying, "Will you not come and sup with us today? We have greatly missed you and Sir James since you found lodgings elsewhere."

John turned to Balfour who was standing nearby.

"Shall we accept this most gracious invitation, Sir James?" he inquired.

"If you are sure that your husband will not disapprove," he replied, "I can assure you that I would be most happy to do so."

"It matters not whether or not he approves," she returned. "There is very little that Marjory and I do which meets with his approbation."

Sir James shrugged his shoulders.

John hesitated for a moment and then replied, "We would not come between you and your husband, ma'am, but if you wish us to do so we shall be happy to accept your gracious invitation."

They, therefore, repaired to the Bowes' home after expressing their thanks to the Monmouths for the use of their great hall.

"It will always be available for these services," Monmouth replied. "It is the least that I can do for freedom."

The dinner at the Bowes' was not a huge success.

"After eating a meal at your service this morning, with both bread and wine, I did not think that any member of this family would be hungry this noon," Richard Bowes remarked. "You did have both wafer and the cup, did you not?"

"Yes, Richard, we had both," Dame Elizabeth agreed, "save for the fact that instead of a wafer we had ordinary bread. We celebrated the Lord's Supper this morning as Protestants should."

"Protestants, h'mph!" ejaculated Sir Richard.

Neither Knox nor Balfour rose to the implied challenge.

"But we *are* Protestants, Richard," said Dame Elizabeth.

"Not I," he returned. "'Tis true that I do not adhere to the Church of Rome but I do give my allegiance to the holy church of which the king is the lawful head and the true representative of Almighty God."

"And that is Protestant, Richard," Dame Elizabeth retorted triumphantly.

"It has nothing to do with Lutheran and Calvinistic heresies and other innovations which came from the continent," he insisted.

"Ah, but it is allied to them," Dame Elizabeth rejoined. "The archbishop and the privy council have invited representatives of those faiths to preach in England and indoctrinate our people with the true faith which Luther espoused and which Calvin continues to uphold."

Marjory interrupted. "Come, father and mother, we have guests this noon," she protested. "Let us leave off this discussion until later."

Mr. Bowes gave his daughter a baleful glare.

"Would you criticize your parents?" he demanded. "And in the presence of others? Fie on you!"

Marjory was not in the least dismayed.

"Messer Knox," she remarked, "would you be so gracious as to grant me an audience this afternoon before you leave, that I may discuss with you grave problems of my soul's salvation?"

"You should not be troubled about your soul, my child," he replied, smiling. "One so gentle as yourself does not need to be anxious concerning God's acceptance of her. But I shall gladly converse with you upon this subject if you will."

James Balfour could scarcely hide his smile.

Dinner over, the company departed amicably from the table.

Marjory led John over to a corner of the great hall where they drew up stools facing one another.

"And now what of thy soul's condition, my child?" asked John.

"Nay, do not call me 'child,'" objected Marjory. "I am a full-grown woman."

"To be sure," he replied. "That is evident. And I crave your indulgence."

"And what shall I call you?" she inquired. "Should you be called Father, being no longer a priest? I should not like to call you Father."

"No," he replied, "nor would I want you to. Call me John, for that is my given name."

She smiled triumphantly.

"Yes, John," she agreed demurely.

"Now what of thy problems?" he inquired.

"I had wondered if mayhap I had been doomed to perdition. I sometimes have exceedingly wicked thoughts and, if I do, will not a just God condemn me for them?"

"All of us at times harbor evil thoughts in our minds," he replied. "There is a constant struggle within our souls 'twixt good and evil. Satan and God contend within us for the mastery. God does not punish us for having evil thoughts. We are punished only for yielding to them."

"Ah, but sometimes I yield to them," she said. "I have a sharp tongue. I am oft impatient. On occasion I get angry."

"That seems to be the experience of many of us," John agreed. "And it is evil so to do. But if you pray sincerely to the Lord He is ready to forgive your sin and cleanse you from all unrighteousness."

"And what if He has foreordained me to perdition? What can I do about that?"

"God has not foreordained anyone to perdition, Marjory," Knox replied. "True, He has given us the choice between good and evil and there are some who deliberately choose evil but God, from the beginning of time, before ever you or I were born, did not decide that either one of us should be damned eternally."

The conference continued for some time. John had never dealt thus with a young woman's problems nor explored the mind of such a person and it was a new experience for him.

When, finally, Marjory had revealed her most pressing problems and could think of no others, John and Sir James departed.

"She is a person of considerable spiritual insight and hungry for the truth," John remarked as they set out for their lodgings.

"I am certain that she is," Sir John drily agreed.

5

John Knox continued to preach in the Monmouth home every Sunday, but during the week he made his way to other cities and towns in the area. After a time he was preaching almost nightly and holding conferences with the clergy and influential laymen during the day.

His Berwick services were finally held in the church after the bishop noted that most of the people who had previously worshiped there had gone to the Monmouth home. Tonstal disliked Knox even more than he had before but he was an eminently practical ecclesiastic. If this was what the people wanted it was what they would get.

Knox made a slight modification in his celebration of the communion. He had preferred that the people should be seated when they received the elements but it had been the custom for long to kneel to receive the wafer. Knox insisted that all should receive the cup as well as the bread but indicated that, while in his opinion it was preferable to receive communion while one was seated, there was no objection to accepting it while kneeling if one did not thereby imply worship or adoration of the elements.

He was as vigorous as ever in his preaching and he condemned sin in every walk of life without regard for persons. Especially was it noted that his preaching was having considerable effect upon the soldiers and sailors who for long had given the authorities in the city many problems because of their roistering on the streets and in taverns.

"If he can make Christians out of them surely there must be some good in the man," some of those who had criticized him most severely began saying.

Wherever Knox found sin he struck out against it. He condemned the nobles for their failure to support the Reformation and for their callous disregard for the welfare of tenants on their estates. He condemned shopkeepers for charging exorbitant prices for their goods. He lashed out against workmen for dawdling at their tasks. For these words of condemnation he could always find a text of Scripture which would fit the needs of his messages and he quoted long passages from Holy Writ.

His sermons were exceedingly vivid. When, in condemning usury, he cited the example of Zacchaeus his auditors could actually see the little taxgatherer climbing up a tree to catch a glimpse of Jesus. When he spoke of the Cross of Jesus Christ people could see, as vividly as if they were actually present, the three crosses on Calvary and those who stood at the foot of the central one: Mary, the mother of Jesus; Elizabeth, her sister; and John, the beloved disciple.

"But where was Peter?" he asked with dramatic intensity. "Where was the man who had announced only a short time before that Jesus was the Christ, the Son of the Living God? Where was the man who had drawn his sword and cut off the ear of the servant of the high priest when they laid rude hands upon the Master in the garden? Oh, that mon was skulking somewhere off in the distance, a-feared to stand by the foot of the Cross.

"And where were the others? Thomas had said, 'Let us go up to Jerusalem that we may also die with him,' but when Jesus was dying on the Cross where was Thomas? He, too, was in hiding. They were like the church in England today. In France and Germany and Switzerland our brethren are ready to stand for the faith as was Wishart in Scotland, and Jan Huss in Prague. But the clergy of this land falter between Rome and Westminster, afraid to take a stand for the Lord."

He and Sir James were still welcome guests at the Bowes' home save for the fact that Mr. Bowes paid them scant heed. However, Richard's opposition was becoming less vocal. He did not attend the services at which Knox preached but he did not voice his disapproval of the preaching to either Knox or Sir James.

Knox found Mrs. Bowes a wise counselor in most things. But she had so many spiritual ailments that she wearied him with her constant requests for advice.

The most frequent request which she put forward was for counsel concerning the manner in which she could win her husband to the Reformation. Knox had suggested that she should not attempt to force him to make a decision.

"Give the mon time," was his constant plea. "Give him an example of Christian living to touch his heart. Show him that one who loves the Lord and seeks to live by His precepts is different from one who does not and he will change."

On the other hand, when she sought counsel regarding her marital obligations and her relationship with Richard, Knox turned her questions brusquely aside.

"With fifteen bairns ye surely know more about that than I do with none," he told her. "How can I advise ye when I have had no experience at all?"

"But you were a priest," she objected. "You have heard confessions."

"Aye," he agreed, "but none to compare with those that ye bring to me now."

Marjory was somewhat like her mother in her desire to reveal her inmost secrets to John, but they were of a different nature. She explored with him deep theological questions which indicated that she was earnestly searching the Scriptures.

Referring to Paul's letter to the Philippian Church, she inquired, "How could Jesus divest Himself of all of His rights and privileges as the Son of God to become a man? And how, if He were the Son of God, could He actually have known suffering upon the Cross? And if He did not suffer there then how can we say that He was the Lamb of God slain from the foundation of the world?"

Patiently John would reply to all of her interrogations.

"With God all things are possible, Marjory. We must ken that Jesus was the altogether pairfect Son of God but that He was likewise altogether the Son of Man. Linked up in His being are God and man. Jesus was both in One. The Son of God hung upon the Cross but Jesus was also the Son of Man and it was the man, Jesus of Nazareth, who suffered there. Never forget that."

But while John and Marjory conversed on various theological subjects he was becoming more and more conscious of the fact that she was also a woman. Nor could she see the bent back and gnarled hands. With a young girl's fancy she began to picture him as a knight in armor, a crusader seeking to wrest the Holy Land from the clutch of infidels.

While John was preaching in the church she hung on every word that he uttered, and John himself was always conscious of her presence in the congregation.

One day Sir James bluntly inquired of him, "Why don't you marry the girl? 'Twould make a good union. She has a mind fit to match your own, and she has health as good as her mother's. Such a marriage should result in many fine children."

"Nay! Nay!" objected John. "Marriage is not for me. I am at the beck and call of the king and the council. I am not settled in any one place. 'Twould not be honorable to marry one who has lived her entire life in one house. She could not be content with the kind of life which I must lead."

"Let her make the decision, John," urged Sir James. "That is the only fair thing to do."

"She is too young to know what it would mean," John replied.

"Young in years, perhaps, but old in experience and mature in her judgments," Sir James reminded him.

Despite his vocal objections John admitted to himself that Marjory attracted him as no other woman had ever done. In addition to his inexperience, however, the disparity in age between the two presented a real obstacle. Marjory was not yet twenty. He was nearing forty. He had no earthly goods. And the stipend which he received from the crown for his preaching barely sufficed to meet his own needs.

He weighed all of these factors, but outweighing them was the fact that he had discovered an emotion which he had not previously realized existed in him — the love of a man for a maid. In her presence he was suffused by a warm glow of well-being. It was as if, before he had met her, he had been only half a man. Now he was becoming whole.

To rid himself of his thoughts for her Knox plunged into a series of outside preaching appointments. When he was away from Berwick he was not as grievously tormented by his affection for the lass.

He began by preaching in near-by towns and villages. At Norham on a Monday night the parish church was filled to capacity to hear him. Word had come from Berwick of his effectiveness as a preacher and everyone who could possibly be present repaired to the church to observe the thunder and lightning which were reputed to play about his head when he preached. He spent a week in Norham, preaching every night and holding conferences during the day.

On Friday night he held a communion service. There wasn't a vacant pew in the church as Knox began his preaching and during the administration of the elements there was not a dry eye among those who were present.

The pastor of the church, Malcolm Wingate, remarked to him afterward, " 'Twas a great experience, Messer Knox, one that neither I nor my people will ever forget. Never again will I withhold the cup from the congregation. From this time forth when we celebrate the Lord's Supper 'twill be as we observed it this night. You must come again and teach us more about the real meaning of the Eucharist and the Protestant Reformation."

Knox was not received as cordially the following week in Anscroft. Michael Cargreen, the pastor, was evidently afraid of Bishop Tonstal and still attempted to balance Rome on one shoulder and the Protestant Reformation on the other. With a divided allegiance he did not know exactly where he stood.

He was evidently in considerable awe of Bishop Tonstal and would do nothing which could possibly offend him.

After every sermon he would add a word of explanation to his congregation, seeking to temper what John Knox had said by watering down his utterances. After his Wednesday evening sermon in which John had greatly criticized the clergy for failing to give wholehearted allegiance to the Protestant cause Cargreen remarked that he knew that Knox referred to only a few clergymen in some place remote from the north of England. The clergy of the Berwick district were men of the highest character and completely loyal to the church.

"To be sure," he added, "we follow the rites of the Mother Church but we yield to no one in our loyalty to the crown."

"I would that ye did not add your own interpretation to what I say," Knox objected later. "I have no need of an intermediary 'twixt myself and the congregation. And I would have ye know that there are more clergymen who are outside of the Reformation than there are men of courage who espouse it. I meant what I said, mon, about the ministers. And one of the chiefest of those who give only lip service to the crown and the Reformation is your own Bishop Tonstal."

"A great and good man!" ejaculated Cargreen. "A loyal Englishman and true to the church!"

"Aye, but which church?" queried John drily.

At the communion service all of the people accepted the bread although some did so with an expression of distaste, since he served ordinary bread and not the wafer to which they were accustomed, but he noted that when the cup was passed many looked up to note the expression on the face of Cargreen. When they saw the storm clouds which sat upon his brow most of them passed the cup to their neighbors without putting it to their lips.

"On the next Lord's Day we shall observe the sacrament in our customary manner," Cargreen, tight-lipped and pale, announced when the service was concluded, giving John a glance of pure malice when he did so.

John was ready to make a sharp retort but thought better of it. At the conclusion of the service, instead of spending the night in the lodgings to which he had been assigned, he packed up his few belongings and set out on foot for Berwick. Once outside Anscroft he took off one shoe, shook it, and replaced it on his foot.

To himself he muttered, "I'm following y'r instructions, Lord. I'm shakin' the dust off my feet when I depart from a place which does not receive either you or me."

Gradually Knox began to go farther afield in his preaching, crossing the northern reaches to Newcastle, Carlisle and Maryport. Everywhere he went he found both clergy and people ignorant of the real meaning of the Reformation. Most churches still adhered to the customs of the past. Many priests still heard confessions and in most of them the mass was celebrated.

Knox found that many of the priests were actually unaware of what had happened in England. They assumed that the death of Henry VIII which had occurred years before had resulted in the return of the church to the sovereignty of Rome. Some of the older clergymen still resented the confiscation of the monasteries by the crown when in 1534 and 1535 the break with Rome had been consummated.

The laity, too, were ignorant of the changes which had been made. It was also true that many people had little time for, or faith in, the church. If they attended services at all it was because they felt compelled to do so — not because they sought the comforts of religion.

Wherever he went John attracted crowds of people. Tradesmen and farmers came to hear him. Nobles rubbed elbows with common laborers.

A baronet at Carlisle remarked, "I do not like the man. I do not accept what he preaches. But I dare not miss the meetings. He stirs up my antagonism but in any event he arouses me. He is unlike the milksop preachers we have had for so long."

As he had time to do so John Knox worked with Sir James on the new book of common worship which he had had in mind to edit. As they finished sections of the book they sent them to Archbishop Cranmer.

After receiving one section of the manuscript Cranmer wrote:

> You and Sir James have given the Protestant flavor to the volume which has been lacking. If we can receive the consent of the crown and the privy council we shall hope to publish it and make it available to our people.
>
> Continue with your good work as you are able. I hear conflicting reports of your ministry from the clergy in the north but all of them redound to your credit. Shortly I would like to have you go to Newcastle to do there what you have done in Berwick. Your ministry at Newcastle is greatly needed. I shall write you again as to the most propitious time to make the move.

Knox confided the contents of the letter to Mrs. Bowes and Marjory.

Marjory, dismayed, remarked, "But that would mean that you would leave Berwick. We'd not hear you preach any more. You can't go, John. The archbishop can't do that to you."

Dame Elizabeth was equally unhappy but did not express herself as forcefully.

"We would miss you sore here," she said. "Your influence has made a new city of Berwick. You have touched the lives of many people and your preaching has changed the lives of many of the ruder inhabitants as nothing else has ever done."

For some time Sir James had been making inquiries of refugees from Scotland and he had been sending letters to friends in Edinburgh and Glasgow when he was able to find an emissary to carry them. He was eager to return to Scotland but was cautious about leaving England until it was assuredly safe for him to do so. Finally word had come that, while it would be unwise to return to Edinburgh, or to St. Andrews, he could return to Glasgow where he was less well known and find refuge with friends.

He confided his intentions to Knox.

"I'm glad for you, Jamie," Knox remarked, "but sorry for mysel'. I'll miss ye sore."

"It has been a wonderful companionship," Sir James remarked, "and I shall keep in communication with you. And, as ye know, I shall bend all my efforts to make the Reformation in Scotland true and vital."

"But you must exercise caution," Knox reminded him. "As you may remember, one of the conditions of our release from the galleys was that we should not return to Scotland. If you are apprehended 'twill go hard with you. And we can ill afford another martyr for the cause."

"Have no fear, John," Sir James replied. "You are the impulsive one — not I. I shall be as cautious as a middle-aged maiden lady walking alone down a dark street."

John smiled. He could scarcely picture the sturdy Scotch laird in the guise of a timid spinster. But he felt that Sir James, at least, would be discreet. The laird was a realist and he knew that he could be of little use to the Reformation if he were languishing in gaol or again serving as an oarsman in a French galley.

The two took leave of one another and Sir James started off

in a borrowed coach for Carlisle, the border city closest to Glasgow.

On one of his last evenings in Berwick John called on the Bowes family to take his leave of them.

Dame Elizabeth was the first to greet him.

"I must see you alone before you depart," she announced. "I never have a moment with you when you come here but I have many things to discuss with you in private."

Knox hesitated.

"I know of no place where we could be assured of privacy," he replied cautiously.

"No place, you mean, where you could see a lady alone without creating a scandal," she returned with a smile.

"Well, yes," he agreed.

"Then could you not come to our home some morning soon? The children will be at their lessons. Richard will be gone and I can give Marjory some task to occupy her."

"Very well," he replied. "Would tomorrow be convenient?"

"Tomorrow at mid-morning," Dame Bowes agreed.

By this time he was overwhelmed by the Bowes children.

With a smile Marjory remarked, "We know not what we shall do with the bairns . . . you see, I know your fine Scotch word, John . . . when their chief playmate leaves. You must not go to Newcastle, John. 'Tis too far away."

"Nay! Nay!" the children echoed in chorus. "You cannot go, John."

"But I must, dear bairns," John replied. "Ne'ertheless we can have this fine evening together. What shall we do?"

"Let's play galley," one of the boys shouted.

"I want to be overseer," Jaimie, six years of age, shouted.

"No! No!" objected Eric. "You know not how to be an overseer. John Knox himself must take that part."

"Very well," Knox agreed, "but I warn you I shall beat you sore if you do not pull right heartily on the oars."

Each child hurriedly found a stave to be used as an oar and they then ranged themselves in two rows. One of them brought a short stick to John. A narrow length of cloth was tied to one end. There were knots in the other end of the cloth which gave the whole the semblance of the whip with which the galley slaves had been beaten.

"Ah, 'tis a fearsome cruel lash," John remarked. "And I am

a rough and rude taskmaster. Now to your oars, you lazy slaves. Lay on, I say!"

Vigorously they pulled on their sticks.

"Together! Together!" he shouted. "The galley is going in every direction but the right one the way ye pull."

He laid about him in mock indignation with his whip, the children laughing and shouting in glee.

Richard Bowes chose that moment to appear.

"Here! Here!" he shouted. "What is this?"

"Can you not see?" replied Marjory. " 'Tis a French galley, father, and John Knox is the cruel overseer."

"I'll not have it," shouted Richard. " 'Tis a foolish game indeed."

Knox looked ruefully at Richard.

"Indeed it is," he agreed.

"Then why did you engage in it?" Richard demanded.

"John Knox did not suggest it," Marjory replied. "The children insisted. He but fell in with their plans."

Richard sputtered, "But he put the wild notion in their little heads. They'd not have thought of such a thing if he had not told them stories of his marvelous adventures with the French."

His speech ended on a note of elaborate sarcasm.

"I am indeed sorry, sir," said John abjectly.

"Well, then, leave off!" Richard replied.

"We will indeed," agreed John.

Shortly thereafter he took his leave.

The next morning, in response to Dame Bowes' request, he arrived at the Bowes' home about ten o'clock. He found Elizabeth awaiting him alone.

She began at once.

"You know, John, with what affection I regard you," she remarked.

John looked at her in dismay. He was speechless for the moment, bereft of words as a deep blush suffused his face.

Dame Elizabeth laughed.

"Nay, do not be afraid that I shall engage in maudlin sentimentality," she remarked. "I regard you as a son although you are not many years younger than I. But, since I think of you in that light I would have you become my son in fact. That is, if you are so minded."

"But . . . how? What do you mean?"

"If I am not mistaken I have detected in you a growing affection for our daughter, Marjory, and I have noted in her an answering response. She loves you, John."

"But — but — " John began again.

"I know what you would say," she replied. "As a priest you took a vow of celibacy. But you are no longer a priest. The vow is no longer binding. You are free to marry, as you know."

"True," he replied. "Yet Marjory is but a child."

"A grown woman!" retorted Elizabeth. "Old enough for marriage, old enough to bear you children."

"Nay, but she should marry someone more nearly her age."

"If she loves you and no one else?"

"She would get over it. Most young women fall in love many times during their lives. And often they fall in love with men who are much older than themselves."

"Not Marjory. If you love her, John, and I believe that you do, I would counsel you to ask for her hand in marriage."

"But I am certain that your husband would not approve. He would surely not accept me as a son," John objected.

"Rubbish! What matters it whether he approves or not. Eventually he will have to accept you."

"But I should speak first to him. He is the head of the house."

"Sheer folly! He would say, 'No.' "

"But he has every right . . ."

"He has not," she asserted stoutly. "There is a barrier betwixt us as you well know. He would never approve one who is committed to reformation as both Marjory and I are. I would never approve one who believes that we should go cringing back to Rome."

John was silent for some time.

Finally he spoke. "I could not be married now. You can readily see that. The times are too troubled. I have many things to do."

"Granted," agreed Dame Elizabeth. "But you could secure her promise of marriage for the future. She scarce slept last night for thinking about your departure."

"Very well, then. I cannot deny that I love Marjory with all my heart and soul. She is a bonnie lass and one with high Christian principles. But time is pressing. Could I see her, think you, this very evening? Could you arrange that there would be no interruption?"

Dame Elizabeth's smile was altogether conspiratorial.

"You shall see her this very night," she promised.

6

John trod on clouds all the way back to his lodgings. He wished that Sir James had remained that he might share his news with him. His shoulders were thrown back, albeit with difficulty. He felt like a lad of sixteen.

Carefully he chose his garb that evening. It would not do to call upon his beloved in patched and mended garments. He rehearsed the speech that he would make.

"I realize, dearest Marjory, that there is a great disparity in our ages but I love thee with my whole heart, and I would pledge to thee my deepest devotion."

He decided that this was too flowery. But what did one say to the most wonderful person in the world? He could not thunder at her as he would do if he were preaching. He could not write a sermon for the occasion. He could not condemn anyone in the earnest manner which he employed when he was in the pulpit. There was no one to condemn.

He decided on a simple approach. He could say, "Marjory, will you be my wife?" Just that. No more.

Yet, as he considered it, that scarcely sufficed. It was too brief, too unemotional.

But did he want to play upon her emotions, to secure an answer from her merely because his eloquence could be persuasive? If he had only had some experience in the matter! But the rugged life of his boyhood, his training for the priesthood, had ill prepared him for love-making.

Still, he had no desire to make the proposal so matter-of-fact that Marjory would think that marriage to John Knox was merely an affair of convenience for him. It was definitely not that. It could not be. He realized now how tender was his affection for her, how greatly he yearned for her companionship and love.

The matter unresolved, he set out tremulously for the Bowes household. For a time his feet seemed unwilling to move. Then his steps speeded up and he walked along briskly. Again, as doubts began to assail him, he went more slowly, almost dreading the moment when he would enter her presence.

Finally he came to the door of her home.

He lifted the great brass knocker resolutely. Then quietly he released it without knocking. He needed time . . . time . . . . But he had no time. The issue would have to be met this evening. He lifted the knocker again and vigorously beat a summons with it.

The gate-keeper came out of his little cottage.

"Oh, Messer Knox," he said, "ye may go right in. They're expectin' you."

For a moment John felt trapped. There was now no turning back. The die had been cast. Marjory would not have been expecting a proposal of marriage but her mother would. He would have to go through with it — no matter what the result.

Never had Marjory appeared more lovely than she did this evening. Her dress was of some soft material, the color of which seemed to enhance the deep blue of her eyes. John had had no experience in describing women's apparel. He was no courtier to make pretty speeches. The feeling that he experienced was one of awe and wonder. Suddenly he knew what it meant to be overwhelmingly in love.

"I'm . . . I'm glad to see you this evening, Marjory."

She laughed, and the sound of her laughter was like a mountain brook, rippling, vibrant, sparkling.

"For the great John Knox that is a most uneloquent speech," she remarked mischievously.

John doggedly began, "I've come . . . I mean I'm here . . . ."

"That is most evident," Marjory suggested demurely.

"Could we not find a . . . er . . . quiet spot where we may converse?"

"Upon the state of the nation, the progress of the Reformation, or the prospect of war with Spain?" she inquired innocently.

"Nay, Marjory, do not jest. I have something important to confide to you."

Impulsively she put her hand on his arm. He thrilled to her touch.

"I am sorry, John. I suspect that it is that little devil in me . . . or you may consider him one of considerable size . . . that makes me do and say such terrible things."

"There is no trace of the evil one in you, dear Marjory," he objected. "You are the gentlest . . . . Aye, thou'rt an angel if ever I knew one."

"I think we had better find a quiet spot," Marjory hastily remarked.

She led him over to a corner by the huge fireplace where they settled themselves on a bench.

"And now what would you confide to me?" she inquired.

"It . . . it is somewhat difficult to know where to begin," he remarked.

"Shall I have to do it for thee?" she inquired innocently.

"Do what for me?"

"Ask me to be thy bride. Was that not what you had in mind?"

Aghast, John did not know how to reply.

"Mother said that that was to be thy purpose in coming," she announced demurely.

Finally John found his tongue. "Aye, it was," he agreed, "but I had hoped to lead up to it by degrees."

She clapped her hands.

"Oh, but you must do so!" she ejaculated. "Tell me what is in your heart and how greatly you love me and how you want me to be your wife and how you will treat me with kindness and great consideration, never beating me if I should disobey your commands, and so on, and so on."

John broke into laughter.

"Ye took the words right from my mouth, lass," he observed, "but I'll not agree to refrain from beating you. From every evidence of your character that I have had I would say that an occasional beating might be a good thing for you. But let that be. I would merely remark for the moment that I love you with all my heart and would have you to wife. I am not worthy of thee but I do love you and would cherish you dearly so long as I live."

"No woman could ask for more," Marjory replied.

There was an awkward pause.

Finally Marjory remarked, "Is not something missing, John? Have you not forgotten that which always seals a troth?"

"What do you mean?"

Her answering blush was a rosy sunset.

"Oh, John, at preaching you are a veritable lion, but at love-making you are altogether a little woolly lamb. I mean a kiss, of course. Or do you not know how such is given and received?"

Now John's cheeks became carmine.

Both stood up. Tentatively John enfolded Marjory in his arms. It was a new experience to him but a delightful one. He discovered one impediment, however. His aquiline nose was in the way, but by tilting his head slightly to one side he managed to implant a kiss upon the lips of his beloved, lips as virgin sweet as violets growing in a shaded dell.

Within himself there was a sigh of deep content but he did not allow the sigh to escape his lips.

Finally Marjory gently disengaged herself.

"Perhaps we had best . . ." she remarked tentatively. "Some of the family might come in, you see."

"Ah, but we should let them all know."

"No! No!" she protested. "Father would be furious. Only mother must know."

"Yes, and she knows already."

"Yes. She knows already."

They were silent for a space of time, gazing the while into each other's eyes.

"And it may be some time before we can be married," she remarked, hoping as she did so that he would say that delay was unnecessary.

"I am afraid that it will be," he agreed.

"But I so much want to be married right now," she added.

"Even more so I," he said, "for I have fewer years of life left to me and I would spend them all with you if I could. But we must be patient."

"Yes, we must be patient," she echoed doubtfully.

"Aye," John added without enthusiasm.

"You will write me when you're in Newcastle, and wherever else you go?" she asked wistfully.

"As often as I can find a messenger to carry a letter to you one shall be on its way," he promised.

At this moment Dame Elizabeth entered the room. She looked at both of them expectantly but for the moment neither had anything to say.

Drily Dame Elizabeth remarked, "From the evidence imprinted on your faces it would seem as if something momentous had been decided. Come, have you nothing to say?"

Marjory looked to John for an answer. He looked at her expectantly.

Finally John spoke.

"Everything is decided," he said, "save the date of the wedding."

"Would that it could be soon," Dame Elizabeth remarked, "but we know that is impossible."

"It will be hard to wait," John said. "I had thought beforehand that I wanted time but now that it is decided I am altogether impatient. If I had my way in the matter we would be married tomorrow."

"Thou'rt as eager as a sixteen-year-old lad, John," Dame Elizabeth remarked.

"I am sixteen years old in my heart," he replied.

"So I see," she said.

"And I am fearful that while I'm absent some handsome swain will come along and pluck my rose," he said.

"No fear of that," Marjory assured him. "I love only thee, John. Never could I love another."

"Yes, I am certain of that," Dame Elizabeth agreed. Turning to Knox she added, "And you have important work to do, John Knox, but the time will come when you can settle down in one place and by then Marjory will be ready to undertake her part in your task. In the meantime I shall teach her all of the arts of being a housewife so that you shall never have cause to regret marrying her."

"Were she to become the poorest housewife in all England I would love her still," John replied fervently.

"That may be your judgment at the moment," Dame Elizabeth rejoined with a smile, "but eventually you would be unhappy with a slovenly helpmeet if she were to be such."

John and Marjory exchanged glances, assuring one another thereby that no matter how much one or the other might lack they would still be sustained by their love for each other. Dame Elizabeth caught the exchange. She remembered that this, too, had happened to her in the early rapture of the love which she had exchanged with Richard but eventually it had worn thin.

Elizabeth acknowledged to herself that the fault was as much hers as it was his. If she could have been a more obedient wife, if the question of religion had not divided them, then indeed might their wedded life have been happier. But Richard was a man who took positive stands on every issue and she recognized the fact that she, too, was inclined to espouse a position in a most decisive manner.

She was to be put to the test again for Richard sensed that something had happened and Marjory's radiance was such that she could not contain her joy. When her father queried her concerning the reason for her seemingly irrepressible happiness she divulged to him its source.

"John and I are to married, Father," she said. "We love each other dearly. To be sure, we realize that we cannot be married immediately."

Richard's brows almost met over the bridge of his nose.

"To be sure," he commented sarcastically.

"Since he must preach in Newcastle for some time and he does not yet have a settled position," she explained, "we cannot well be married now. But soon he will be able to locate in one place and then we can be united."

"Oh, you can, eh?" he demanded. "But what about my permission? Why did not your precious John Knox come to see me to inquire if this proposed marriage met with my approval? Does a father in these modern times have nothing to say concerning the person to whom his daughter is to be espoused?"

"But Mother approves," Marjory replied.

"Oh, to be sure, Mother approves," he returned, mimicking her words. "Anything that misshapen mountebank suggests she approves. She approves of his preaching. She approves of his mission to upset the church. She approves of his diatribes against the established clergy and the nobles. She has been completely under his spell since he appeared in Berwick. But he doesn't meet with my approval. Not by any manner of means! And he never will."

"We hoped that when you came to know him better you would look with favor on his suit," Marjory suggested.

"Never! Never! Never!" Richard shouted. "And I want him never more to cross the threshold of my home. Is that clear?"

"It is," Marjory acknowledged, "but do you care naught for my happiness, father? Do you desire that I remain a spinster all my years?"

"Spinster, hah! There is no danger of that," he replied. "You are young. Men will find you desirable. In but a few years you will have more swains than this house could contain."

"I want only one," she insisted, "John Knox, the man to whom I am betrothed."

"Well, I forbid the marriage. I forbid you to see him again or have aught to do with the man. He shall never set foot in this house again. I do not want to see the fellow again — now or ever. Had he not been at one time a priest, and were he not still a clergyman of sorts, I would call him out and run him through."

Marjory, tight-lipped, left the presence of her father and sought out her mother.

"He is cruel, cruel, cruel," she sobbed. "He cares nothing at all for my happiness. For some reason he hates John Knox passionately. And John is the gentlest soul I have ever known. True, in the pulpit he seems austere, commanding. But underneath all that is the real John, tender, earnest, warmhearted. Would that father could see that too. You see him so, do you not, Mother?"

"Yes, my child, I do. But your father considers him a man with no virtues whatsoever. Your father can nourish a strong hatred and such is his feeling for John. But we do not need to be disturbed about that now. It will be some time before you and John can be married. Time is on our side."

Dame Elizabeth sent word around to John's lodgings concerning what had transpired. She wrote,

> Marjory and I are not greatly concerned because of my husband's opposition. I had not intended to tell him of your betrothal to Marjory but her sweet face revealed her happiness and she thought that because she was so happy her father would share her joy.
> But he did not. He has forbidden you the house. But do not be dismayed thereby. I can always arrange, when you come to Berwick, that Marjory shall meet you somewhere. No doubt the Monmouths, since they are such warm friends of yours, would be delighted to have you see Marjory in their home.
> Yet I think for the moment, until Richard has had time to cool off, that it would be better if you did not try to see Marjory again. To be sure, she would like to see you every day, every hour, but Richard would be sure to know about the meeting and it would only disturb him anew.

John had no intention of seeing Marjory again. First of all, he was overdue at Newcastle. He must hasten to meet appointments which had been made for him. Second, he desired to savor his new-found joy before he added to it new moments with his beloved.

The church in Newcastle was within the jurisdiction of Bishop Tonstal but Tonstal was notoriously lazy and strongly averse to travel. It is doubtful, therefore, if he ever visited this parish. Knox found it exceedingly fertile ground for his preaching. Newcastle was much more of a center of commerce than Berwick and exceedingly independent in spirit.

Ready for his leadership was a young associate, Henry Whitworth. Whitworth had gone to the continent in search of light on the meaning of the Reformation and, while he and Knox differed in many points of theology, their differences were in matters of interpretation and not in spirit.

"It is good to welcome you to Newcastle," Whitworth said cordially when Knox met him. "Our people are ready for you. They are true adherents of the Reformation and I understand that you had many difficulties and much opposition in Berwick."

"That I did," Knox agreed, "but thanks be to God, before I left Berwick the church became altogether established in the Reformed movement."

"Despite the bishop?" Whitworth remarked.

"My labors did not altogether meet with his approval," Knox replied drily.

"I'd not expect that they would."

On the following Sabbath Knox preached in the church. Again he launched into a sturdy defense of the Protestant movement. The papacy, he insisted, was not a Biblical institution. He noted that when Jesus said to Peter, "Thou art Peter, and on this rock I will build my church, and the gates of hell shall not prevail against it," He did not refer to Peter as one who would become a pope in the church which was yet to be founded in Rome. Instead, he referred to Peter's confession in which the apostle had said, "Thou art the Christ, the Son of the living God."

Peter had had much to do with the establishment of the church but Paul, the missionary apostle, had probably done much more than Peter. Peter had been instrumental in founding the church in Rome but he had built upon the foundations which Paul had laid during the years of his imprisonment there. The church at Rome was only one of many churches, each being equal parts of the whole.

He denounced the mass as unscriptural and insisted that Jesus had instituted the Lord's Supper — not the mass — as a memorial feast in which all could participate, laity as well as clergy.

During the course of the sermon he noted what for him must have been a strange phenomenon for the people were nodding their heads in agreement. When he had preached for the first time in Berwick his words had been greeted by many with scowls and much shaking of heads in disapproval. Whatever he said in Newcastle seemed to meet with the approbation of the congregation.

Before the service closed the communion was celebrated by Whitworth but the young man gave both elements to all of the communicants.

"As I have told you before," Whitworth announced, "and I say to you again, the prayer of the institution of the supper does not change the bread into the body of Christ. Nay, it still remains bread. The prayer did not change the wine into Christ's precious blood. It remains wine. But Christ is present with those elements and as you partake of them ye become identified spiritually with the death and sacrifice of our blessed Master. Eat and drink for as often as ye do so ye do show forth the Lord's death 'til He come."

After the service people greeted Knox warmly. There was not a single word of disapproval of his message. No one challenged his right to preach. Accustomed to controversy, Knox was almost disappointed at his reception. At the same time he was heartened by the welcome and warmed by the good will of the people.

Later he went to the humble home of Henry Whitworth and partook of the simple repast which Marcia, Henry's wife, had provided. The Whitworths were the parents of five children, the eldest being eight years of age.

"Were you a priest?" Knox asked him bluntly after they had partaken.

"No," Whitworth replied. "I was studying for the priesthood but before I could be ordained the Reformation was on. Most of my fellow students were unhappy about it but I had had serious doubts of my calling and the Reformation resolved them for me. I joined up with it even before we declared our independence of Rome. I was among the first to receive ordination at the hands of Archbishop Cranmer. When he laid his hands upon me in ordination – without the use of holy water – he pointed out that I was ordained by the Church Universal and not by the Church of Rome."

"And then you went to the continent to study, did you not?" Knox inquired.

"Yes, I went to Marburg. I wanted to study under Martin Luther but he had died only a short time before I arrived there."

"But you believe with Luther that Christ is present *with* the elements in the communion service?"

"Aye," Whitworth replied. "Do ye not also?"

"No," John replied judicially. "At least not in the same man-

ner that Luther believed. 'Tis difficult to explain the difference
— and 'tis not of great importance — but I believe, as does Calvin,
that the communion is a sacrament of remembrance. Christ is
present in the communion but not *with* the elements. He said,
'This do in remembrance of me,' so He is present but in a memorial capacity."

"I see," Whitworth said.

"Nay, I am not sure that you do," Knox remarked, "but it little
matters. We will not quarrel about it. There will be those in
the church who will accept Luther's interpretation of the sacrament and those who accept Calvin's but they will stand
shoulder to shoulder in their defense of the faith. And I would
not have you change your mind to conform to my own thinking."

"But I shall want to hear more from you concerning this,"
Whitworth replied. "I had heard of this difference but did not
rightfully understand it."

"As I say, it matters not, but I shall gladly interpret Calvin's position for you if I can. This I must say, although I am glad
that I can serve here with you, so far as I can see there is little
that I can do in Newcastle which has not already been done. You
have so well indoctrinated these people that there is little I
can add. I shall be free, therefore, to preach elsewhere, knowing that with you here in the pulpit these people will receive
the bread of life."

For two months, however, Knox continued his preaching in
Newcastle and held many meetings on weekdays in the homes
of the people of the parish. He found them eager and interested
in his teaching.

Early in 1552 he received a call from the archbishop to come
to London. The young king had heard so much of John's preaching that he was eager to have him come to the city so that he
might hear him himself, and Cranmer wanted to discuss with
him the proposed revision of the Book of Common Worship.

Knox announced to the congregation one Sunday morning that
the king had commanded him to come to London. "But you
will not miss me," he added, "for your young minister is so thoroughly grounded in our Protestant faith that his preaching will
be good for your souls. He and I do differ on some points of
interpretation of the Scriptures but they are minor. And each one
of us must interpret the teaching of our Master in the light of

our own consciences. Henry Whitworth's faith is rooted and grounded in love. I am sure that when Paul used those words he described that which animates the preaching of my young brother in Christ."

7

Cranmer took Knox into his own home when Knox arrived in London.

"I have much to discuss with you," the archbishop said, "and later we can arrange for you to have a room in the chapter house or in the palace."

"In the palace?" exclaimed John. "What do you mean?"

"The young Edward has had great curiosity concerning your preaching since he has had word concerning you," the archbishop explained. "In light of the fact that you are one of his chaplains he desired that you should come and preach in the palace chapel."

"But I have just begun my work in Newcastle," John objected.

"And would not be able to leave it?" Cranmer asked.

"No. I could not honestly say that," John replied. "Henry Whitworth, the young minister of the church, seems to be well grounded in the Protestant faith. You may remember that you ordained him yourself. Truly, I am not needed in the pulpit there at all but there are other towns in the countryside where my services may be of value."

"Nevertheless, probably not as important as ministering to the king," Cranmer remarked drily. "Edward is a youth of exceedingly pious disposition. Naturally there are influences at work seeking to win him to the Roman position. We were fearful when Somerset fell that the Duke of Northumberland would seek to gain the king's support for the Roman Church.

"The duke is a cold man and we did not know just where he stood but he has been even more vigorous than Somerset in some of his decisions. His very first official act after he became protector was to ban images. Within a short time he placed a ban on altars. This has done more to discourage ministers who would like to celebrate mass than anything that has happened."

Edward was only fourteen years of age when Knox began preaching in the palace chapel. Knox's own frailties endeared him to the young king who likewise suffered ill health. Edward was a precocious individual, eager to learn and possessing a brilliant mind. Knox's preaching fired his imagination. He was thoroughly committed to the Protestant cause which his father, Henry VIII, had espoused in order to rid himself of one queen, Catherine of Aragon, and marry another, Anne Boleyn. Edward was the son of Henry's third wife, Jane Seymour, and was the only male child of lusty Henry VIII.

He had acquired from his father a doggedness in reaching and holding to decisions but this characteristic was tempered by his mother's gentleness.

The young king was sincerely Protestant but there was little appeal for him in the milk-and-water sermons which he heard regularly in the palace chapel. Yet when John Knox began preaching the young king paid him the closest heed.

He had never before met John, although he had appointed him a chaplain in ordinary, until the Scot electrified him and stirred his imagination by his dynamic preaching.

In his thick Scotch burr Knox spoke directly to the monarch.

"Ye are king by divine right," Knox announced. "That is true. But whomsoever God appoints and anoints to a task is also a servant. Our Lord Jesus Christ, possessing a divine right greater than that which any earthly monarch possesses, the right of birth as the Son of the Eternal God, said, 'I am among you as one that serveth.' Thus, also, are kings anointed by divine right to be servants of Almighty God and to serve their people.

"If they are not willing to accept the responsibilities of their high office then they are not fit to serve. I charge you to remember always the needs of your people, to pray Almighty God that you may be a wise and good king, and, forgetful of self, to do for your people that which is for their welfare."

The young ruler gazed up at John Knox transfixed.

Knox had not thundered. He had not condemned. But he had touched a boy's heart.

"I must meet him," he whispered to the Duke of Northumberland. "Why have I never heard him before?"

"Ssh, your majesty," the Duke replied. "We can talk of that later."

John was commanded to dine with the king following the

service. He accepted the summons with no particular qualms. For him there was one King only to whom he owed allegiance, the Lord Jesus Christ. Earthly monarchs, to his way of thinking, were ordinary human beings, and this particular king was just a spindling lad.

"Why is your back so rounded?" Edward asked him as they were seated at the table and John's posture appeared to him as that of an old owl seated on a limb high up in a tree.

"Your majesty," chided the duke. "It is not meet to ask such a question."

"Nay, your lordship," protested Knox. "I do not mind. My back became this way, your majesty, when I was taken prisoner by the French after the capitulation of St. Andrews in Scotland. You see, I spent nineteen months chained to an oar in a French galley. In truth, I have rowed almost the length of the Mediterranean sea and between many ports in the Atlantic. I had a comrade, Sir James Balfour, a fellow prisoner, who was much more rugged than I was and accustomed to living much of the time out-of-doors. His body does not exhibit as does mine the marks of his imprisonment. But a scholar's bones are much softer than those of such an one as Sir James."

"But why did the French take you prisoner?" King Edward inquired.

"In order to destroy Protestant resistance in Scotland," John Knox replied. "St. Andrews was the very center of the Reformation movement there."

"P'tah! Those wily French!" the young king exclaimed. "Some day I hope to start a war with them and when I do we'll beat them roundly."

Again Northumberland intervened.

"We must guard our tongues, majesty," he reminded the monarch. "To be sure, 'tis all right to speak thus in the presence of John Knox for he has suffered much at their hands but we must be careful not to express ourselves in this manner in other company."

"But, uncle, there is no other company present save yourself; and I am sure that you would not inform the ambassador from France of my future intentions."

Northumberland shrugged his shoulders slightly and favored Knox with a half smile.

"Are you a married man?" the king inquired of Knox.

"No," John replied. "But I have the promise of a young lady

in Berwick, one of your majesty's loyal subjects, that some day she shall become my wife. But first I must establish a home somewhere. At the moment, as your majesty is aware, I travel too much on your majesty's behalf to be able to have a home."

"Have her come to the palace. You can live here and always be my minister," Edward proclaimed.

"A capital idea," Northumberland remarked, "but your majesty decided some time ago that Knox should preach in our church in Newcastle and in many of the surrounding towns. He will be engaged in that activity for some considerable time still."

"I did decide that?" asked Edward.

"Yes, indeed," Northumberland replied.

"Well, revoke the decision," said Edward. "We need John Knox here."

"He will be with us for some time," Northumberland reminded him, "but your majesty would not want Newcastle to relapse into Romanism. And there would be danger that it would do so if Knox were to come to London permanently."

Edward pursed his brow.

"I suppose there would be," he agreed. "Still, whilst thou art here with us, John Knox, I would that you should continue to preach on the duties of a king. I am over-young to realize what they should be."

"You honor me, sir," John replied.

In the weeks that followed the king had many conversations with John. Knox sensed a loneliness in the lad which touched his heart. The king was surrounded by courtiers who flattered and cajoled him and quite evidently he had little stomach for their words. John was kindly but honest. He did not hesitate to outline for the king how he thought that the king should conduct himself.

"One thing especially ye should remember, majesty. You must be the king of all of your people. Young as you are, they regard you well-nigh as their father. You should get out among them, mingle with them, learn what their problems are, their heartaches and their joys. So will you earn their love — and that is much more important than their respect or allegiance."

Thus John advised the king on one occasion.

"But how can I go out among them? I'm always surrounded by members of my court."

"Ask the duke how to arrange it. He will know the way in which it can be done."

"I will," announced the king decisively.

On another occasion the king wanted to know what his position was in respect to the church.

"One of my titles is 'Defender of the Faith.' What do I do to defend the faith?" he inquired. "That sounds as if 'The Faith' has enemies."

"Indeed it has," Knox assured him. "'The Faith' to which your title refers is the true religion of our Lord Jesus Christ. In your coronation you agreed to defend that. If you would be a true king you will not allow foreign heresies to creep into your nation. You will not permit ecclesiastics of a foreign power to dictate what your people shall believe. The nation broke with Rome during the realm of your father but many of your clergy still long for the days when the Roman pontiff dictated what they should believe and how they should conduct themselves. You must defend your church from clergy who yearn for the fleshpots of Rome."

"I shall defend the true faith with my life," the young king replied passionately.

Cranmer arranged for Knox to give a series of lectures to members of the clergy. They could not very well absent themselves in view of the fact that the king himself made it a point to attend all of them. However, Knox found an eagerness on the part of most clergymen to learn more about the Reformation and its meaning.

They had accepted the fact that they were no longer in communion with Rome but many of them had not realized what a reformation involved. They still clung to the practices of that which had been their mother church. Questions at these meetings would come thick and fast.

"Why have we given up the confessional?" one inquired.

"Because it is not Scriptural," John Knox replied.

"But did not Saint James command that we do so?" the man returned triumphantly. "He said, 'Confess your faults one to another.' Is that not confession?"

"Aye," John returned, "but it is not the confessional. If I have wronged you I should go to you and acknowledge my guilt, and ask your pardon. That is all that the Scripture writer meant. And all of the rest involved in the confessional, the remission of sins by a priest, and the exaction of a penance — these are not to be found in Saint James' pastoral letter."

"But what if I shall never see again the man whom I have wronged? To whom then should I go to confess my sin?"

"Go to our Lord Jesus Christ. You need no intermediary between Him and yourself. But you can also go to some other person. However, that other person need not be a priest. He can be any friend or counselor."

"But the confessional box is a practical means of making confession," the man still argued. "The priest does not see the confessor. Confession is made in secret."

"Ah, but is it?" John countered. "The voice betrays one. I heard many confessions in my time. I did not know the voices of all who confessed their sins to me but I knew many, and it gave me a power over them that no man should possess. The abuses of the confessional have been many, as you well know."

He added, "In truth, the confessional is an adaptation of the ancient practice of oracles, a heathen custom entirely. And the confessional box is similar to the niche occupied by the oracle in a heathen temple. Supposedly a disembodied spirit occupied the cubicle. But such it was not for there was a hidden entrance through which the pagan priest entered and if he did not know the identity of the one who had come to him for a prediction he could readily slip out afterwards and discover who it was who had appeared.

"Nay, the confessional is not Christian. It is one of the many heathen practices which were superimposed upon the church in its early days. And the mass was like it in that the bells and incense were part of the heathen rigmarole of ancient sacrifice."

Cranmer nodded his head in agreement.

King Edward listened to every word.

There were those among his courtiers who scoffed at John Knox and sought to influence the king against him but the king's privy council openly supported the Scotsman. In any event the young king accepted the teachings of Knox and took them to heart. More and more he was grounded in what he believed to be his mission as a king.

Finally, however, Knox felt that his work at the court was finished and he should return to Newcastle.

"We have done little with the book on which we were to have worked," Cranmer suggested. "Would it not be wise to remain here longer and spend some time on that?"

"But I am so busy while here in London that I seem to have

little time for it. Would it not be better to return to Newcastle where I am not always interrupted?"

Reluctantly the archbishop agreed.

"Yes, perhaps it would. But you will continue to send me your thoughts on the matter?"

"Gladly," Knox replied.

"And I suspect that you are also eager to see the young woman to whom you are espoused?" Cranmer suggested slyly.

Knox smiled ruefully.

"Is my affection for Marjory so apparent, then, to all?" he asked.

"No. Only to me," Cranmer replied.

Shortly thereafter John took his leave of the king.

In the short time that he had been in London John had become fond of the young monarch. Frail though he was in body, he seemed to possess all of the attributes which John felt should be possessed by a king. His heart went out to the lad for he sensed that the boy was animated by a tremendous desire to serve God and his kingdom.

"You will keep me informed of the progress of thy work for me and for the church?" the king inquired wistfully.

"Assuredly, your majesty," John replied. "And I shall pray daily that you may be given strength for your task and the good health to continue to serve for many years.

"And you will pray that I may be a good king?" the young monarch continued.

"I shall do so most certainly," John replied, "and since that is such a strong desire on thy part I am certain that God will answer our prayers."

"I pray that He may," the young king remarked fervently.

The king himself provided a coach for John and sent him on his way back to Newcastle. As John rode along the highway and observed the awe with which people stepped aside as the royal equipage passed, he recalled his experiences in the French galley.

"Forgive me, Lord," he prayed, "for I have been near to becoming prideful, rejoicing in the vanity of horses and a carriage."

As a penance for these thoughts he almost decided to send the coach back and continue on foot, but practical considerations triumphed. It would take him several weeks to make the

journey on foot and a matter of two days to make it by coach
and he wanted to reach Newcastle at the earliest possible moment. And, after all, it was not *his* coach.

8

As soon as Knox arrived in Newcastle he sat down and in-
scribed a letter to Marjory. He explained,

> I would have written to you earlier but I was so occupied
> in London that I scarce had time for my prayers. And I am,
> indeed, a poor writer of letters. Then, for a time, I was quar-
> tered in the palace and our young monarch was so eager to
> hear more concerning the Reformation and his own responsi-
> bility for the progress of the movement in the church that I
> did not have a moment which I could call my own.
> Again, I could not be certain, if I wrote a letter that it would
> reach your own precious hands and I would not have an epistle
> of mine read by one other than yourself. Now I write to assure
> you of my undying love. And I would also assure you that I
> am looking forward to the time when we may be joined in
> marriage. Your mother described me as a sixteen-year-old
> boy. In my eagerness to see you and my yearning for you
> I am such without a doubt.
> But I must keep my eagerness in check. I must learn to be
> patient and to wait. The king himself desired that I should
> be married at this time and come with you to live in the palace.
> It was a tempting prospect but one from which I had to turn
> aside. The Reformation must reach the people in the small
> towns and the countryside, and I am equipped to carry it there.
> I am convinced that if our people up and down the land can
> be won to the cause it will be firmly established. The king
> and his privy council can do much — indeed, Edward is doing
> much, despite his youth — to secure the benefits of the Refor-
> mation for England. Yet the people must be informed and,
> as I have traveled up and down among the villages and towns
> of the country, I find the most woeful ignorance among them
> regarding the purposes of the movement.
> Assure your dear mother of my unfailing love for her. Were
> it not for her counsel I should never have had the courage
> to ask thee, to be my wife. I should have been altogether
> frightened by your father's opposition. But our separation
> from one another has only deepened my love for you and my
> determination that we shall one day — soon, I hope — be
> united. With sincere love,
>
> Y'rs respectfully,
John Knox

The letter was placed in Marjory's hands by a refugee Scotsman who was traveling north to the border. John had coun-

seled him to see that the letter was delivered only to Marjory herself or her mother.

The Scot had winked and said, "I shall be a cloth salesman. I'll take my samples right into the house. I'll see that y'r epistle gets into her own fair hands."

He was as good as his word.

When he appeared at the Bowes' home he told the gate-keeper that he had hand-woven wool cloth from the backs of honest Scotch sheep and he was eager to let milady view for herself the tremendous bargains which he had to offer.

"Be off with you," the gate-keeper commanded. "Mrs. Bowes will buy her cloth in the market."

"Ah, but she asked to have me come," he said. "A man by the name of John whom I knew back in Scotland told me that she would be interested in fine woolens and I have some of uncomparable worth which she'd be delighted to view. I have made a long journey especially to offer them to her."

Grumbling, the gate-keeper dispatched a footman to the house with the message.

Dame Elizabeth seemed to be uninterested but finally said, " 'Twill do no harm to see his goods. Let him come."

When the Scot appeared he inquired, "Do ye have a daughter, m'lady?"

"I have many daughters," Dame Elizabeth replied.

"But one especially by the name of Marjory?" he continued.

"Ah," she agreed. "Yes, I do."

"Perhaps she, too, would be interested in my cloth," he suggested.

Mrs. Bowes smiled.

"I am confident that she would be," she said. "I'll go call her."

When Marjory came into the room the Scot remarked, "I have a special cloth for you, m'lady. There are no tartans anywhere in the world as those from the highland district. They have a distinct weave and patterns that will suit the most fastidious taste."

He unrolled a piece of cloth and surreptitiously slipped the letter into her hand.

"Have you ever seen anything the like of this?" he asked.

Marjory smiled at him.

"The pattern is not exactly what I have wanted," she said, "but the weave is beautiful. Perhaps when you come again you could bring other patterns to show me."

Casually she placed the letter in her bodice.

"Ma'am, you have a most discriminating taste," the Scotsman remarked. "Ye can be sure that I shall return with other patterns which are more to y'r liking."

"If you would be so good," Marjory agreed with a nod.

"And you, m'lady," the Scotsman said, turning to Dame Elizabeth, "do you see nothing in this stock which merits your approval?"

"The cloth is excellent," she replied, "but there is nothing that I can use now. But, as you say, possibly when you return from Scotland you may have something which would interest us. Will you be back soon?"

"I'm on my way to Scotland the noo," he replied, "and I'll come by, the Lord willin', on my return."

Marjory read her letter eagerly as soon as she reached her room. Emerging, after she had read and reread the epistle, she sought out her mother and, assured that no one else was nearby, read the letter to her.

"He has been living in the palace, Mother, my John has. No less. Imagine that! That should win Father over to us."

Dame Elizabeth shook her head.

"If he hath been living in heaven itself I don't think it would influence your father."

"What shall we do then when it is time for us to be married? Will I have to run away with John?"

"We can wait until that time comes," Elizabeth replied. "Time effects many changes. A way may be found then of which we have no present inkling."

John went ahead with his busy preaching schedule, going farther and farther afield, but conducting the services in Newcastle whenever he was there. He continued his correspondence with Cranmer concerning the Book of Common Worship and finally saw the volume published. It was not entirely to his liking but it embodied many of his ideas and in considerable measure the language of the volume was John Knox's.

The book soon saw widespread use and both Cranmer and Knox had cause to believe that the people of England understood much better the meaning of Protestantism by virtue of what they read in the printed word. Although he would have changed many sections in it John was sufficiently realistic to understand that such a volume could not embody all of his thinking. By its very nature it would be a compromise.

Cranmer had used as much of the material which Knox had supplied as he possibly could but he understood the temper of the clergy much better than Knox did. He realized how fast the Reformation movement could proceed and how far it could go. But the friendship between the English ecclesiastic and the Scot grew apace and Cranmer saw to it that Knox often preached at Westminster.

John's last sermon to be preached in the Abbey was in April, 1553. The previous Christmas he had been deeply stirred by word which had come to him to the effect that some of the clergy were interested in a plot to secure the overthrow of the king. He had preached a sermon in Newcastle shortly thereafter in which he charged the clergy of the land with treason.

"Touch not the Lord's anointed," he had thundered during the course of the Newcastle sermon. "When violent men plot against the monarch they plot against the Lord. God will bring to naught their evil plans for He cannot give His blessing either to nobles or clergy who would overthrow him whom the Lord has set over this fair land as its monarch.

"May God pity them in their blindness and bring all their cruel schemes to naught. They not only conspire against the person of his majesty but at the same time they conspire against God Himself.

"They plan for the overthrow of the church which He has graciously blessed. They would enslave our minds once more and enslave our persons as well. I know what slavery is. None better than I. Would you exchange your liberty for the chains of Rome?"

None of the people in Newcastle had been involved in the plot but so stirring had been John's denunciatory message that news concerning it had traveled the length and breadth of the realm. Cranmer asked him to come to London to inform him concerning the plot which he had mentioned but Knox was able to give him little news concerning the manner or place of its inception or those who were engaged in it. Apparently the plot was merely one of those sporadic movements which develop through whispering campaigns. But John's sermon served to arouse the countryside against the danger in which the king constantly stood.

The king also wanted news concerning the plot and again

sent word to John that he would like to have him come to London as often as he could. Thus it was that he had preached in the Abbey early in January and had been scheduled for service the following April when the king heard him again.

Once more Knox prayed for God's guidance for the young king, for a long and useful reign, and that England might prosper spiritually and materially.

"You always give me new heart and courage," Edward remarked to John the following day. "I know that I am over young to reign but almost you make me believe that I can."

"Ye are doing well, majesty," Knox assured him. "May you increase in strength and grace in the years to come that y'r reign may be one richly blessed of God."

But even as he spoke these words Knox wondered if the young monarch would ever reach manhood. He looked pitifully frail.

The following July sixth beacon fires were lighted all over England and the news was flashed by swift couriers to every part of the realm that the king had died. John was in Newcastle at the time but he hastened to London. He sensed the fact that the capital would be in turmoil and that the question of a successor to the monarch would be of tremendous importance to the Reformation movement.

Arriving in London, he sought for news of what was happening from friends but received only guarded replies. When he conferred with the Archbishop of Canterbury Cranmer said, "All the information that I have indicates that Edward will be succeeded by Mary Tudor. If that occurs it will mean hard years ahead for the church. The gains which have been made during Edward's reign will all be lost. I know that I shall soon be replaced if that happens and it may well be that I shall go to the stake. We shall know soon."

"But why will she be chosen?"

"Because she is next in line for the throne. We are a nation of traditionalists. Our people have come to believe so staunchly in a royal line that it matters little whether or not a monarch is equipped to reign. Mary is ill suited to her task of ruling a nation committed to the Protestant cause. She is fanatically Roman Catholic. She is married to a Spanish prince and we would become in effect a vassal of Spain. Would to God that Elizabeth had been the next in line instead!"

"And what of my work?" John inquired. "Shall I continue preaching?"

"Assuredly not," the archbishop replied. "The first thing that Mary will do upon her accession will be to replace all of the king's chaplains with men of her own choosing — or probably with one chaplain only. And he will be a Spanish priest, I doubt not."

"Then I had best return to Scotland?"

"No. Scotland is in worse plight than England. The regent is French and you would be a marked man. No! My counsel would be, go to the continent. Go to Geneva or Zurich and wait this out. That is the only safe refuge now for Protestants."

"But I do not seek my own safety," Knox returned.

Cranmer gave him a wry smile.

"Do you think, John, that you can be of greatest service to the cause if you are rowing again in a galley or incarcerated deep in some dungeon? Will you serve the cause of God best by going to the stake?"

"I do not fear such a fate."

"I am aware of that, but we have had enough martyrs. We need living messengers, preachers who, when the change inevitably comes, will be ready to step into the breach. I say that it is not a matter of what you would wish for yourself but of what is best for the Kingdom of God. Get out of England, John. Go as fast as you can."

Heavy of heart, John left London and returned to Newcastle. He bore tidings of these events to the leaders of the church there. He told them what the archbishop had advised regarding his own situation.

His friends counseled him to leave as soon as he could possibly do so, and they set about arranging for his passage across the North Sea to some port on the coast of France, preferably a smaller town where he would not be in danger of being apprehended. John agreed to leave but suggested that he should wait until they had news of the actual accession of Mary.

"But what will you do?" John asked.

"We shall continue to worship God as we have been doing," Henry Whitworth said, "but I know now that we shall have to do so in the privacy of some home."

On July nineteenth the event happened which they had feared. Mary Tudor was proclaimed queen. John dispatched a letter to Marjory advising her of his decision to go to Switzerland.

"Perhaps, when I arrive there, I can send for you and we can be married," he wrote, "but I have no assurance that such will be possible. I yearn for you with all my heart and I trust in God's own time that we may become one flesh and one spirit. Thine own John."

This letter was dispatched by the same Scotsman who had carried his earlier missive. He appeared once more in the guise of a cloth merchant but this time received an immediate warm welcome by Dame Elizabeth.

"I bear good tidings concerning John Knox," he said to her, "but ye may consider them sore. For he has had to flee to France. With Mary on the throne it would not be safe for him to remain in England. He wanted to stay but we persuaded him that we did not need more martyrs to the cause. We need livin' preachers and when England repents of the folly of invitin' this Spanish queen to occupy the throne he'll be needed here again. He was still in Newcastle when I left but they were arranging for his passage."

"Thank God, he is safe," Marjory remarked when she heard the news, "but when will I see my John again? Mother, do you think that we will ever be married? We have encountered so many obstacles that I have begun to despair."

"Never doubt, my dear, that John Knox and the good Lord will find a way," her mother assured her.

However, Knox had not left England as originally planned. Parliament had decided, with Mary's acquiescence, to make a gradual change and had granted Protestants a limited right of assembly and John felt he should stay in England as long as he could. December twentieth was set as the final date when Protestants would be protected in this right.

Parliament anticipated that by that time the Reformationists would have realized the futility of fighting the inevitable and would have returned to the churches which had reestablished the ties with Rome and would worship according to the Roman customs once more.

Mary's proclamation of amnesty for Protestants evidently lulled Knox into a feeling of security for he continued his preaching. He even prayed for the queen, following the ritual in the Book of Common Worship. This he would have omitted, however, if he had not been convinced that the queen would be tolerant of Protestant worship. He was no longer a chaplain in ordinary but he received sufficient funds from his lectures to satisfy his needs and he felt sufficiently secure to contemplate marriage with Marjory at this time.

To this end he had an interview with Richard's brother, Sir Robert Bowes. The results were negative.

He communicated them in a letter to Mrs. Bowes in which he wrote:

> Dear Mother,
>   So may and will I call you, not only for the tender affection I bear you in Christ, but also for the motherly kindness ye have shown unto me at all times since our first acquaintance; albeit such things as I have desired (if it had pleased God), and ye and others have long desired, are never like to come to pass, yet shall ye be sure that my love and care toward you shall never abate, so long as I can care for any earthly creature.
>   Ye shall understand that this sixth of November I spake with Sir Robert Bowes on the matter ye know, according to your request, whose disdainful, yea, despiteful words, have so pierced my heart, that my life is bitter unto me. I bear a good countenance with a sore troubled heart; while he that ought to consider matters with deep judgment is become not only a despiser but also a taunter of God's messengers. God be merciful unto him.

Later he wrote her once more, saying, "It will be after the twelfth day of December before I can be at Berwick; and almost I am determined not to come at all. Ye know the cause. God be more merciful to some than they are equitable to me in judgment. The testimony of my conscience absolves me, before His face who looks not upon the presence of man."

"That means, then, that there is now no hope of our marriage?" Marjory remarked woefully when her mother read the letter to her.

"Not at all," replied Dame Elizabeth. "It means that your Uncle Robert stands with your father in opposition to John Knox and that is all. Never fear, my child. The day will come when you will be joined to John in holy matrimony. I promise you that, so long as I live, I shall strive to bring that event to pass."

"But we have waited so long," Marjory protested, her lower lip quivering.

"You are young, my child," her mother said, "and it is hard to wait before you have lived for many years. But these are unsettled times and almost anything can happen."

But John Knox was not to reach Berwick at this time. If he had gone it is doubtful if he could have seen Marjory, for Sir Robert had alerted his brother Richard and warned him that John would doubtless make an attempt to see his betrothed, and Richard was so determined that Marjory would have nothing to do with Knox that he virtually made her a prisoner in her own home.

In January, 1554, Knox landed at Dieppe on the Normandy coast of France.

Dieppe was overcrowded at this time with refugees from England. Since the deadline for Protestant worship had passed, many other Englishmen, with their wives and families, had also sought to escape to France. Although the French were not favorable to the Protestant cause they felt that by offering English Protestants refuge they could thereby embarrass both the English and Spanish governments so they opened their ports to them.

Most of the refugees made their way from the French ports to Germany and soon English-speaking congregations were set up in Strassburg, Wesel, Emden, Frankfurt and Hamburg. The largest group congregated in Frankfurt. These people had to obtain permission from the city government to secure a place for worship but it was readily granted on condition that those permitted to worship there should not include German-speaking Protestants but only those who had come from England.

John met a great many refugees in Dieppe. It was fortunate that he did so for his sole fortune at the time consisted in the clothes on his back, a few books, a quill pen, ink and some writing paper, and less than ten groats.* But he preached to the refugee group in a cold, dark warehouse near the waterfront and the people insisted on taking an offering for him.

John likened their situation to that of the Israelites in exile in Babylon and Nineveh.

"We, too, shall return at last to our Jerusalem," he said. "Although the homeland is in the possession now of those who have no regard for the religion of our Lord Jesus Christ, the people of England and Scotland have had a taste of freedom. They have learned to think for themselves and no queen will ever be able to force them back into a groove of slavery. We shall return to reestablish freedom in the land of our birth. Having known the fruits of liberty our people shall not long endure under a foreign tyranny."

"Well said, John Knox," a former Cambridge don assured him.

* An English coin of the fourteenth and fifteenth centuries which was worth about fourpence.

"Ye took the very words out of me mouth," a burly Scot informed him. "But when we return to our island, John Knox, ye must go to Scotland. We'll be needin' you there."

"All the years of my exile I have devoutly hoped for that," Knox said with heartfelt earnestness.

9

With sufficient funds in hand to assure him that he could reach Geneva, Knox set out for the Swiss stronghold of Protestantism. He greatly longed to meet John Calvin. Of all the reformers he felt that Calvin had laid hold upon more of the truth than any other. By temperament Knox was closer to Luther than Calvin. Where Calvin parried strokes as with a rapier Luther used a broadsword, and the club which Knox wielded was more like a sword in its effectiveness than a rapier.

But Calvin's theology more nearly paralleled his own, and Calvin was deeply concerned with the question of the form of government which the Protestant church should assume as was Knox. Knox preached to stir up the people to the end that they would demand a government with a climate in which freedom of thought might flourish. He believed wholeheartedly that only so could Reformation gain a foothold in the land. Hence his determination to see Calvin.

But he arrived in Geneva at a most unpropitious time. Before the end of 1554 Calvin was to be endowed with considerable personal authority but he did not yet possess it. He was much too busy to spend any time with a Protestant from another land and the long conferences with Calvin which Knox had visualized for himself did not come to pass.

Knox was also eager to secure Calvin's opinion concerning the relationship which Knox should sustain to the English crown. Was a man justified in seeking to overthrow the authority of a monarch whose reign was not in the best interests of her people? But Calvin was having his own difficulties in the field of government. He did not want to espouse a view which could conceivably be used against him when he sought to set up a government which would be at one and the same time both ecclesiastical and secular, by taking a stand concerning a government in a distant country.

Calvin had learned from experience that it was unwise to make statements which at some later time could be wrested from their context and used against him.

Thus, cautiously he suggested, "I would advise you to go to Zurich and seek out Henry Bullinger. He is well versed in the science of government and he might give you valuable counsel."

"But yourself have had a training in such science which is unequaled among those who espouse the cause of the Reformation," Knox countered. "Could ye not give me answers to the questions which trouble me?"

"What are those questions?" Calvin inquired.

Knox brought forth a paper on which a series of four questions had been set down. He began reading them to Calvin.

"The first is this," Knox read. "Might the son of a king, upon his father's death, though unable by reason of his tender age to conduct the government of the kingdom, be regarded, nevertheless, by right of inheritance, as a lawful magistrate, and as such be obeyed as of divine right?"

John glanced expectantly at Calvin.

"Go on," Calvin suggested.

"The second question is one which concerns the present situation in England. It is: 'Might a female preside over and rule a kingdom by divine right, and so transfer the right of sovereignty to her husband?' That is the present danger faced by the church and the kingdom. In the event that Mary should die and her husband should succeed to the throne we would become, in effect, a colony of Spain."

Calvin pursed his brows in thought. He seemed on the verge of making a statement but finally sighed and remarked, "Continue."

"This is one which is most pressing and it troubles most sorely the leaders of our movement. They are loyal to the government but are uncertain just how far their loyalty should extend. It is: 'Is obedience to be rendered to a magistrate who enforces idolatry and condemns true religion; and are those authorities, who are still in military occupation of towns and fortresses, permitted to repel this ungodly violence from themselves and their friends?' "

Calvin remarked drily, "I can see the dilemma in which they are placed."

"What answer, then, can I send to them which would bear the

stamp of your authority?" Knox inquired. "They need your
personal counsel and guidance."

Calvin's only reply was, "Are there any further questions?"

"Only one," replied John. "This is the one which my friends
would have me ask in the event that another candidate for the
throne could be persuaded to come forward. It is: 'To which
party must godly persons attach themselves, in the case of a
religious nobility resisting an idolatrous sovereign?' "

Calvin rested his chin on his fists, pondering the questions.
He faced a serious dilemma if he made answer to this turbu-
lent Scot. If he declared himself on any of these issues his answers conceivably might rise to plague him when he sought
to erect the government which he envisaged for Geneva. He
was not insensitive to the problems which Knox propounded, but
England was far away. In all probability, even if he declared
himself, his declarations would help the English church but
little. The very fact that one who was by birth a Frenchman
should presume to rule upon issues which were concerns of the
English people and their church might serve to hinder instead
of help.

Finally he made reply.

"I can only reiterate what I said before. Go to Henry Bullinger. I am not qualified to pass upon these questions. It would
take days of historical research — time which I can ill afford to
spend — to give you the precedents which presumably should
govern. No, I am afraid that I cannot advise you. But Bullinger
is a scholar and his advice would be infinitely more acceptable
to your English colleagues than mine."

Knox could scarcely conceal his disappointment.

"Thank you, Messer Calvin," he remarked. "I shall do as you
suggest."

If he had been younger he would probably have challenged
Calvin, have urged him to take a stand. But he recognized the
delicacy of Calvin's position and decided that he would pursue
the matter no further.

Knox went back to his lodgings sore at heart. He had hoped
for a reply which he could use. He was almost resolved to return to Germany to consult with Lutheran leaders but he finally
decided that he would go to Zurich and interview Bullinger although he hoped for little from the patriarch. Constant travel,

too, was beginning to pall. His bent was for action. The times demanded haste.

However, he set out for Zurich, his questions still unanswered by an authority whom he could quote. He had his own answers for the questions but he realized that they were his own and that the English clergy would discount them, knowing his tempestuous nature.

He smiled ruefully. If only he knew how to be politic. If only he had not acquired such a reputation for tempestuousness! Even his friends in England would not accept his authority. They would say, "Of course, that is how John Knox feels, but who is he to tell us what we should do in our situation? What did he accomplish in Scotland by his thunderbolt tactics?"

And so, with little faith that he would learn much from Bullinger, but with Scotch tenacity, he set his steps toward Zurich.

He found Bullinger vastly different in temperament from Calvin. The patriarch was bluff, hearty, a man big in body, friendly, receptive. But Bullinger, too, was cautious. He had heard little concerning John Knox and had had only vague reports of what had occurred in England, and what he had heard did not appeal to him. He accepted the Catholic position that the Reformation movement had started in England as a convenience for a monarch who had sought to put away a wife that he might marry his paramour. He had little knowledge of the earnest spirit of reform which had been prevalent in the island country for a century prior to the break with Rome.

All that Bullinger could recall concerning the rise of the Reformation movement was the much publicized separation of the ruler and his spouse. It seemed to him that this was the important factor in the Protestant uprising there and he mistrusted its motives and its leaders in consequence.

Nevertheless, he lent a willing ear to Knox but hedged his replies with caution. He was just as unwilling as Calvin to set down his answers in writing. Knox wanted a document which he could send to England in which Calvin — or Bullinger — would commit themselves to a position which would be helpful to the English clergy. Actually Knox's confidence in such a document was exceedingly naive. If it had been written it would have had little effect on the situation in England. Mary was resolved to blot out every trace of Protestantism and the mere possession of such a document would have been prima-facie evidence of what Mary would have regarded as treason and heresy.

However, Bullinger did make an attempt to answer Knox's questions.

Knox read, as previously he had done for Calvin, from his written list. The first question, to be sure, was moot. Edward VI was no longer living. But Bullinger hesitated to reply unequivocally to it and he combined the answer with a reply to the second question.

"Messer Knox," he asserted, "it matters not who ascends the throne, whether it be a lad too young to reign or a female. If they come to power through long-established law or custom, their rule will not be challenged by any godly person."

"The clergy did not challenge the right of Edward to reign," Knox replied drily. "True, he did not actually rule in England since a privy council was selected to transact the affairs of government in his name. But I observed the lad take a profound interest in the affairs of the realm and had he lived he would have made a great king."

"Ah, yes," Bullinger replied, bringing his finger tips together.

"The real questions are concerned with the right of Mary to reign," Knox replied.

"To be sure," Bullinger agreed.

"And there is a further question, 'Can she transfer the right of sovereignty to her husband?' He is, in effect, king in her stead. Does she have the right to grant him such broad powers of government? And does the church have the right to resist such sovereignty with all of the strength at its command?" Knox inquired.

"Let us proceed to consider the matter without reference to persons," Bullinger replied. "Let us see if we cannot discover a general principle which would govern in all cases."

"Yes."

"Well, we may set down as a general principle one that is based on Jesus' word, 'Render unto Caesar the things that are Caesar's, and unto God the things that are God's,'" said Bullinger. "You will recall that the Pharisees sought to entrap Jesus, my friend. They put to him a question which, if it were answered in one way, would place Jesus in the position of rebelling against Roman authority. If it were answered in another it would seem as if Jesus were counseling the Jews to deny the authority of God."

"Assuredly," Knox agreed.

"Then my answer to you would be the same as Jesus'," Bullinger continued. "It matters not who is on the throne of England. If the monarch occupying the throne has lawful authority for such occupancy all right-minded people will obey the rule of such a monarch. On the other hand, no one is commanded in the Scriptures to obey man-made laws which are contrary to the law of God. Conceivably, even rebellion might be justified in certain circumstances but only after every other remedy has been tried — and then only after earnest prayer and heart-searching."

"But Mary has forbidden Protestants to hold services. They are expected to return to the churches which now celebrate the mass and other such idolatrous practices. They must go to confession weekly on penalty of a denial of the sacrament and possibly even death."

"Ah, yes," Bullinger replied.

"Under such circumstances what should our English brethren do?"

"I know what you would like me to say," Bullinger replied cautiously. "But put yourself in my place, Messer Knox. I am far away from the situation which you describe. If I try to set down a set of general principles for you — and especially if I commit them to writing — they can be twisted to apply to another set of circumstances. True, I realize that you would not so twist and thwart them but it would be possible for others to do so."

Knox reluctantly agreed. While he would have made a snap judgment himself if he were in Bullinger's shoes he could see and understand the man's point of view. But it was exceedingly disappointing not to receive from him the answers to the questions which he was asking, and Knox realized that he had gained nothing which he could communicate to the clergy in England.

He returned again to Geneva for a further conference with Calvin.

"What did Bullinger counsel?" Calvin inquired.

John gave him the substance of Bullinger's reply.

"Excellent advice," Calvin said. "Excellent."

"But scarcely of assistance to the clergy in England," Knox remarked ruefully.

Calvin gave him a tight smile.

"No," he agreed. "But I am not sure that if he had given other reply it would have served them any better."

"Perhaps not. But I have a question which you may be able to answer for me."

"Yes?"

"Where can I best serve the cause of the Reformation here and now?" John asked bluntly.

Calvin pondered a moment.

"I think I have just the place for you," Calvin finally suggested. "Some English refugees are eager to establish a church in Frankfurt and they have asked me for advice concerning the pastorate of the church. They have suggested that I nominate a likely candidate for the post. I would gladly recommend you if you would be agreeable to serving them. It will give you something to do while awaiting favorable circumstances for a return to either England or Scotland. I know how hard it is to wait. I have had to learn that lesson also, for much of my life has been spent waiting for events to transpire which would make it possible to advance our cause."

"I am not temperamentally equipped to endure waiting with ease," Knox acknowledged ruefully.

"It is a lesson that we must all learn," Calvin emphasized.

"Perhaps I should take time to consider where I may best serve the cause but I am inclined to believe that this is the call of God. Therefore, I shall do as you suggest. But I shall want to return to Geneva from time to time to learn more from you. There is an air of freedom here which is good for my soul."

"If that is so," Calvin replied, "it is because we have waited patiently for the time to come when such there would be."

10

In the fall of 1554 Knox took up his duties in Frankfurt with Thomas Lever of Zurich as his associate. It was the opportunity to which John had looked forward for years. He could now apparently be settled for some considerable period of time in one place. Extensive travel would no longer be necessary.

He was minded to write to Marjory at once and urge her to join him there but caution prevailed. He had better wait until he was assured that he would serve there for some time.

He came to this decision after meeting with the officials of the church. It had been loosely organized on a congregational basis but a responsible group of laymen had been selected by the members to make decisions which could then be referred to the congregation for final action.

The great difficulty which John faced was that the refugees represented many different shades of Protestant opinion. There were those who had adopted an exceedingly high church view. There were yet others who opposed all forms and ceremony in the church. The differences of opinion were focused on the various attitudes which they took toward the English Prayer Book.

The first contingent which had arrived in Frankfurt was a French-speaking group. These were Huguenots who had left France because of the persecution they suffered there, and had settled at Glastonbury Abbey in England during the reign of Edward VI. When Mary came to power they fled again, this time to Denmark, but the Danish Protestants did not approve of their Calvinistic position, and they moved once more, sojourning briefly in Hamburg. The Protestants in Hamburg were equally unsympathetic toward them and they finally settled in Frankfurt.

In Frankfurt two different reformation strains mingled, Zwinglian and Lutheran. The two groups were accustomed to differences of opinion in matters of theology and church government. The city council, therefore, gave them refuge and assigned to them a building where they might worship. Their pastor was Vallerand Pullain.

Two months later the first of the English refugees arrived. They also petitioned the council for permission to stay in the city and worship there. The only building available for services was the one which was occupied by the French Huguenot group. The council offered the English the use of this building jointly with the French but, mindful of the possibility of strife, they decided that the English group would have to subscribe to the French Reformed Confession of Faith.

In order to conform to this provision they would have to modify their English Prayer Book. The clergymen would wear no surplices. There would be no litany and responses. It was no hardship for them to agree to these terms since they represented the group of English Protestants who had gone farther than any others in their separation from Rome.

One of their leaders, William Whittingham, had been in close touch with Calvin and with continental Protestants and he knew the spirit of the Reformation movement in France and Switzerland. It was he who, with the consent of the other members of his group, had written John Calvin to ask him to recommend someone to minister to them.

He and John Knox became friends immediately. Whittingham took Knox into his own quarters for a time until Knox could find lodgings of his own.

John's preaching now took on a different note. He sensed the homesickness of his congregation and his sermons, although they were exceedingly long, were full of assurance for the refugees. He was not preaching to a congregation of worshipers who were resisting the Reformation as had been the case in England: He sensed that he was preaching to people who had been willing to suffer for the cause.

The bond which developed between him and his little flock was exceedingly strong. For the first time in his experience, since he had left the priesthood, he became a shepherd of a flock and no longer a crusader for reform.

He spent much time in becoming acquainted with the families in his parish. True, he was also exceedingly busy preparing his sermons. His addresses in England had been semi-political in nature and required considerably less preparation, since they came out of burning convictions, than the sermons which he now began to preach which were intended to comfort and build up hope and faith in his hearers.

As he called in the homes he became acquainted with children and young people as well as adults and it opened up to him a new world of service and opportunity.

It was a fresh experience for him to dandle a child on his knee but one which gave him a keen sense of yearning that he might some day have children of his own.

"He's a sturdy bairn," he remarked to one housewife, the spouse of an English professor.

She smiled proudly.

"Much more like a farmer's child than the son of a school teacher," she remarked.

"Ah, but he has his father's fine brow," Knox reminded her.

"But look at those hands," she said. "Did you ever see such broad fingers and such a wide palm as the babe possesses?"

"They almost match mine," Knox remarked. "You're certain he never pulled oar on a French galley?"

"I'm certain that he didn't," she replied laughingly. "I can account for almost every moment of his life since he was born."

He discussed marketing problems with others.

"I think that the storekeepers charge us double what they do their German customers," one housewife remarked despairingly.

"Learn to bargain with them," John advised. "Say, *Zu viel,* which means, 'Too much.'"

These were probably the only two words in the German language about which he could be absolutely certain but he applied himself to a study of the language and soon was fairly proficient in communicating with his German friends. The gutturals in the German tongue appealed to him, for his own Scotch burr was similar to their speech in many ways.

There were many new faces in the congregation every Sunday morning and afternoon. But there were as many different ideas regarding the conduct of worship, the use of the Book of Common Worship, and theology as there were different groups represented.

"We came here to find freedom," Knox told Thomas Lever. "These French Protestants have divorced themselves entirely from the Romanist past but many Englishmen still cling to portions of it. We should use the prayer book of the French church which Calvin has accepted and approved."

"Nay, but these people are accustomed to our English work. Why should they accept that which is foreign to them?"

"We promised the city council that if we could use this building, sharing it with the French congregation, we would subscribe to the Reformed Confession of Faith," Knox insisted.

"But their prayer book is not a part of that," Lever retorted.

"The French prayer book is based upon it," Knox replied.

Others joined in the controversy.

Relations between the two men became strained.

Finally, early in January, 1555, John wrote to Calvin, outlining the situation. He asked Calvin if it would not be better for him to resign his post and return to Geneva than to remain in Frankfurt. William Whittingham joined with him in writing the letter.

Calvin replied later in the month that he had read the English prayer book and there was much in it that he did not understand, and portions which he could not approve. He could not say that he could accept it without qualification.

"However, Brother John," he wrote, "it is much more important that the brethren in the Frankfurt congregation should learn to dwell together in unity. You are all Protestants. You came to Frankfurt to escape the persecution of a tyrannical English queen. It would indeed be regrettable if that which separated you should be certain ceremonies of mere human invention. Controversy is the very thing that we must avoid.

"Would it not be possible to work out some compromise with your friends — I am sure that you account them as such — whereby you can worship and work together in peace and amity?"

William Whittingham jumped to his feet at the meeting where Calvin's letter was read.

"I propose that we work out an order of worship which will be acceptable to all of us," he suggested. "I would further propose that we use this order of worship until Easter at which time we can make additional revisions if they seem advisable. Messer Calvin has given us a basis for service together upon which all reasonably minded Christians can unite."

John stepped over to him and warmly shook his hand.

"Spoken like the true Christian brother that you are, William," he exclaimed. "As Saint Paul said, 'Who can separate us from the love of God? Shall tribulation, trial, nakedness, or sword? Nay, in all these things we are more than conquerors through Him who loved us. For I am sure that neither death, nor life, nor angels, nor principalities, nor things present, nor things to come, nor powers, nor height, nor depth, nor anything else in all creation, will be able to separate us from the love of God in Christ Jesus, our Lord.' I shall gladly enter into such a compact with you."

They immediately began to work upon such a service and before the meeting was over they had devised a program for their worship which was agreeable to all. The meeting broke up with expressions of good will from all sides.

Thomas Lever remarked, "I shall write immediately to John Calvin to inform him of the happy results of our meeting. I know that he will be overjoyed to learn how amicably our deliberations have been concluded."

A new spirit immediately prevailed in the congregation. Whether Lever preached or John Knox took the pulpit it was as if the Spirit of God spoke through the man.

"Thomas," Knox remarked to Lever, "as you know, I have never been one to compromise when I thought that I was in the right. I have been justly charged with being inflexible, never yielding an inch. But I can say now, in good conscience, that in matters which do not involve vital principles Christians must learn to yield to one another. More than ever I regard you as the good Christian brother that you are."

This was the spirit which was abroad in the congregation until a new contingent of refugees arrived. The group was headed by Richard Cox, one of the principal authors of the English prayer book. He had been the chancellor of the University at Oxford and had been called, not without reason, "the Cancellor."

This group arrived en masse in Frankfurt and immediately joined with the congregation in the Sunday service.

But the service was barely over when Cox was heard to mutter, " 'Twas no service at all. It lacked dignity. 'Twas a skeleton with no flesh and blood. How that Scot can call this Christian worship is more than I can understand."

His spirit communicated itself to his entire group and they all turned away dissatisfied.

Knox called upon Cox the following week. He sought to explain to him what had happened in the congregation before the arrival of Cox and his company, the difficulties which they had faced, and the happy results of their compromise.

"Are we to be dictated to by a pipsqueak of a Frenchman?" Cox retorted. "What is the name of your so-called eminent authority?"

"He is John Calvin who, before he espoused the cause of Protestantism, was a leading professor at the Sorbonne," John explained. "England has derived much good from his teaching. Much of the theology of our church for the past ten years was based upon his thinking."

"Our church!" exclaimed Cox. "What do you mean? The Church of England or the Church of Scotland? You know full well that your church in Scotland is no longer Protestant. And you are no Englishman. You merely lived among us on sufferance. You are a foreigner."

"Yet we speak the same language. We are of the same race. Our people have had much in common throughout the centuries," John Knox replied.

"We seek not the domination of either Frenchman nor Scotsman in our English church," Cox retorted.

"You know my reputation," John replied. "When have I ever sought to dictate to the English church?"

"You tried to write our prayer book."

"I merely supplied to the Archbishop of Canterbury, at his request, material which he thought might be of service in its composition," Knox explained. "You yourself had much more to do with it than I did."

"Cranmer! Bah! He's a tired old man, easily influenced by any mountebank."

A sharp retort rose to Knox's lips but he refrained from uttering it.

"I would not quarrel with you, Brother Cox," John said, "but I would remind you that we had a happy congregation here until you came. Immediately upon your arrival you began to stir up dissension. Can we not learn to worship together despite our differences? Is the Protestant church to be split into numerous segments like a beheaded snake, each piece of the church denouncing the other, each one seeking to outdistance the other?"

"The Protestant church must stand for the truth," Cox shouted. "It must not be laden with heretics. It must not lay hold upon various heresies."

John realized that Cox's definition of a heresy would be anything which deviated from his own form or practice. It became evident to him that further conference with Cox would be fruitless.

"Since your group feels so differently from the one which we have established here would it not be best for you to find another place in which you can worship according to the light which you yourself have received?" suggested John. "You cannot hope to change our way of thinking. We would not seek to change yours."

"It is our mission to change the world — beginning here," Cox retorted.

At the service on the following Sunday bedlam ensued. During the litany there were jeers and catcalls. Not even the prayers were exempt from interruption by members of Cox's group.

Knox had intended to preach a non-controversial sermon but he quickly changed his mind, preaching, instead, like the firebrand who had carried the Reformation story to the towns and hamlets of England.

His sermon was a stirring denunciation of Cox and his friends.

"Ye are like the Judaizers who dogged the footsteps of the great Apostle Paul," he began. "Ye have come among us to stir up dissension and trouble. Not all of us have thought alike. We have had our differences, but we have been living together as Christians. We have composed our differences. We have worshiped together as friends. But you have come here to foment strife, to stir up enmity. That is not the Protestant way to worship God: that is not the Christian way.

"The genius of our Protestant faith is that each of us may worship God according to the light of his own conscience. But that does not mean that we must force all people to believe as we do. I have no desire that you who have lately come among us should believe as we do concerning the nature of the Eucharist.

"I would not have you depart from any tenet of the faith which you hold to be essential. I only plead with you as fellow Christians to accord to us the courtesy of conducting our services according to the light that is given to us. If you are not happy in our services you can always arrange to conduct your own at another time and place."

Throughout his message Cox's followers interrupted, jeered at the Scot, stamped their feet and otherwise interrupted. Immediately upon the conclusion of the service Richard Cox arose in his place and announced, "We petition the membership of this church for admission as fellow Christians."

Now it was the turn of Knox's friends to interrupt.

"No! No!" they shouted. "Let them go elsewhere. Let them find another place for their meetings! We want them not!"

Knox sympathized completely with them. But a principle was involved. These people, albeit they were troublemakers, sought admission to the membership of the church as fellow Protestants.

John held up his hand for silence.

"My friends," he said, "I feel as you do that there is such a wide gulf separating those who have recently come to Frankfurt and have sought today to disrupt this meeting from those who have here found fellowship and friendship through service together, that the chasm cannot be easily bridged. But who am I to stand in the place of Almighty God and say to them, 'Ye cannot join with us because you are not of us. Ye cannot become a part of this group because you do not view the Christian Church in the same light that we do.'

"The very genius of Protestantism is that we stand together despite differences. We must admit these people into membership because they, too, are Protestant. Luther viewed the Christian message in much different light from that which Calvin does. Zwingli put a still different interpretation upon the meaning of faith. One hundred years ago Jan Huss emphasized other facets of Christian doctrine. Yet scholars have gone from Germany to Switzerland, from Paris to Prague, and have worshiped with each group. That is where the Protestant church stands. That is where we must stand."

One of Knox's group, a much-respected professor from Cambridge, Daniel Hammer, white-bearded, saintly in appearance, arose and asked to speak. Knox recognized him.

"I stand with John Knox," he said. "I have been exceedingly happy with his leadership. I have worshiped here with great joy. For the first time in my life I have felt that I was a free man, free to think for myself, free of authoritarianism. But I believe, as he does, that we must accord to these newcomers the right to express themselves, the right even to jeer at our mode of worship. They have introduced the note of dissension, but we must recognize the right of dissent although we would wish that they would exercise that right in much different spirit than they have shown. Nevertheless, I am for admitting them to full rights in this congregation."

There were groans but when the matter was put to a vote Cox's entire company was admitted into membership in the church.

John and Daniel Hammer walked away from the service together.

"We have opened the way to trouble and dissension, John," the old professor said.

"I know it," John replied. "It seems as if the church is doomed to difference of opinion, to hopeless division and confusion."

"It is incidental to the birth pangs through which we must pass. The early church had the same experience," Hammer remarked. "And when those differences disappeared and authoritarianism replaced them the church became what it was when we broke with it. We must guard against authoritarianism and even encourage dissent."

"Aye, that we must," Knox conceded.

Richard Cox apparently decided that Knox had taken his stand out of weakness and immediately set about the task of winning over the rank and file of the membership to his side. This was not too difficult since many of the people were piqued with Knox for not taking a firm stand against Cox. Forgetting the fact that Cox was the cause of the disturbance, they threw in their lot with him and several weeks later a motion was passed forbidding Knox to preach.

Although John and William Whittingham had had their differences of opinion, this action was too much for the latter. Without consulting John — for he sensed that John would oppose his action — he went to the city magistrates. He pointed out to them the conditions under which the English congregation had originally been permitted to worship in the building. They had subscribed to the Reformed Confession of Faith and adopted it as their own.

"I can assure your excellencies that the group which has taken control of our English-speaking congregation will not agree to accept it," Whittingham asserted.

"If that is the case we must issue an order forbidding any preaching whatsoever," one of the magistrates remarked. He looked to his colleagues to ascertain their views. They nodded their heads in agreement.

The next Sunday Cox arrived triumphantly at the church, intending to take the pulpit himself; but a representative of the magistrates was present. When the service began he stepped dramatically forward.

"Stop!" he exclaimed in German. "It is forbidden today to conduct services."

Cox paid no attention to the interruption.

"In the name of the emperor, stop!" the man commanded once more. He stepped forward to the pulpit and waved the order under Cox's nose.

Cox accepted the paper, opened it, read it through, and then announced, "It seems that some of the members of the congregation have secured an order from the city magistrate forbidding us to meet this morning. I regret to say that the service must terminate but I can promise you that we shall not yield abjectly to this order. We shall appear before these same magistrates ourselves and inform them of the character of the individuals who have secured this writ. It must not be permitted to stand."

"What did he mean by that?" John asked Whittingham after the service.

Both had been in attendance — not because they approved of Cox but because John felt duty bound to be present at a worship service — no matter who conducted it.

Whittingham was silent.

"And who secured the order from the magistrate?" John continued.

When Whittingham did not answer John asked quietly, "Did you, Will?"

"Aye," Whittingham replied dejectedly. "That I did. Mayhap it was a mistake but I could not stand idly by and see you maligned, and everything that we had built up here destroyed by that upstart. But possibly it was a mistake to take the matter to law."

"That it was," Knox assured him. "If we Protestants take such a matter to court — and especially those of us who belong to the Reformed movement — we bring ourselves into disrepute not only among the Roman Catholics but with our Lutheran friends as well. This we should have avoided."

"I am indeed sorry," Whittingham remarked abjectly.

However, the fat was in the fire. Richard Cox, with a group of his supporters, appeared before the magistrates. Cox had a weapon with him which was a most potent one. Knox had earlier written a pamphlet in defense of the English Reformation in which he had assailed not only the pope but the emperor of the Holy Roman Empire as well.

The pamphlet had not been circulated on the continent but it had had widespread circulation in England. Cox brought this pamphlet to court.

"May it please your excellencies," he said, "I have here a tract written by this John Knox who had been preaching in the church until our group appeared. In it this fellow has attacked the emperor who had so graciously given refuge to our English Protestants. He has abused the hospitality of his majesty."

"Be so good as to give us the copy of the tract," one of the judges requested.

Cox brought the pamphlet to the bench and gravely handed it to the principal magistrate. They passed it gravely from one to the other. None of them could read it but all of them nodded their heads. The magistrates were Lutheran and sympathetic to the Reformation cause but they had no wish to become involved in a quarrel between the emperor and a group of Protestants other than their own.

The magistrates had not been favorably impressed by Cox but had liked the straightforward manner of Knox and Whittingham, but this was not their quarrel. They did not want to be put in the position of deciding favorably toward one who had attacked the emperor, particularly in view of the fact that he was then sojourning in Augsburg.

Having brought forth his potent weapon, Cox and his group triumphantly left the chamber. Whittingham and other friends of Knox, who had been present for the hearing, remained.

The president of the council cleared his throat.

"We have little sympathy for that man," he said to Whittingham, "and we have been very much pleased with the conduct of your people. You worked in harmony with the French congregation and gave neither them nor us any trouble, but you can understand the situation in which this places us. We would not rule in favor of Messer Cox but we shall be forced to do so if John Knox is the issue. As between Knox and Cox we would have to decide in favor of Cox."

The friends of Knox hung their heads in dismay.

"If you could persuade John Knox to leave . . ." the magistrate began tentatively.

"But his ministry has been so helpful," one of John's supporters protested. "He has given us faith and courage. Until this . . . this upstart appeared we were most happy in our church. Now he has brought dissension and unhappiness."

"It grieves us . . ." the magistrate began but did not finish his sentence.

Whittingham searched the faces of every member of his group. Despair was written on every countenance. Finally he spoke.

"We shall consult with Messer Knox. I am sure that he will go when he understands the issues that we face. But we regret the necessity which forces him to make such a decision."

"We, too," the magistrate echoed.

That evening the group met with John.

"You understand our predicament," Whittingham remarked.

"That I do," Knox agreed, "and I shall make plans to leave at once."

"But we do not want thee to depart," one of the group explained unhappily. "Can we not wait this out?"

John smiled.

"So long as I remain I shall be a source of contention. It is for the good of the church that I go. While this accusation of treason which Cox has made hangs over my head you will be condemned with me as traitors. 'Tis for the good of the church that I depart," he said.

On March twenty-fifth well over fifty friends of Knox met in his home to bid him farewell. Knox made it the occasion for a brief message. He reminded them of the passion and resurrection of Christ and recalled Paul's words that unless Christians were ready to suffer with Christ they could not inherit the crown which the Lord had laid up for every true believer.

"I would be prepared to remain here if it would profit the church," he said. "But we know that it would avail little for me to go to trial at this time for treason. And the church is strong today. There are those among you who will not allow it to get into the hands of its enemies. You will be able to defend and preserve it if you do not at the same time have to defend John Knox."

Reluctantly they acquiesced and the next morning a large company of them set out with him on the way to Geneva, resolved that they would, at least, provide for him an escort for a short distance along the road to the city on the lake.

11

At noon the company shared their lunch. It was a balmy spring day and the group disported themselves merrily, hiding their heavy hearts.

"You will keep us informed of your progress in Geneva?" Whittingham inquired.

"You can be assured that I shall most certainly," John promised.

The company toasted their friend with goat's milk and then took leave of him.

John set out briskly. Despite the fact that the farewells had been sorrowful his heart overflowed with joy. He would now be able to sit at the feet of John Calvin and find answers to some of the questions of Biblical interpretation which still disturbed him. And Calvin might be able to assist him in settling the knottiest problem of all, that of the form which the Protestant church should assume.

If it were to be a church of the people then the government should be in their hands or in those of their elected representatives. But how could one set up a church which would be well governed if the power resided there? Ordinary people were so fallible, so easily moved by their emotions. But if they did not possess such power would it not be possible for some especially strong-willed individual to impose his authority upon the church? And if that occurred would not the end result be merely a faint copy of the Church in Rome?

In many respects that seemed to be the knottiest problem of all.

Like to it, however, was the question of the relationship between the church and the state. What relationship should one sustain to the other? Should the church be subordinate to the state? God forbid! But should the church dominate the state? That was equally intolerable.

The afternoon sun was warm. Fleecy clouds scudded across a blue sky. Early flowers, wild blue hyacinths, snowdrops, and primroses bloomed in every field. John's spirits soared as he walked on.

He was buoyed up by the thought of possible conversations with Calvin. Doubtless the scholar secretly yearned to be a man of action. Calvin undoubtedly must have longed at times to have the forthrightness and physical stamina of Knox, for the latter, despite his frail body, was essentially tough and durable, made so, in part, by his experience in the French galleys. But Knox was just as eager to possess Calvin's ability to solve knotty questions of doctrine and church government, to understand and be able to analyze, as Calvin was, the multitudinous factors which confronted him.

Knox regarded Calvin as the statesman of the Reformation. He thought of Geneva as the fountainhead of Reformation wisdom. He was, therefore, grateful for the opportunity to return to Geneva to study under Calvin. On his earlier visits to the city Calvin had been so preoccupied with many problems which had pressed him for time that his interviews with Knox had been sketchy indeed. But Calvin had finally secured the reforms which he had sought and he had been able to set up in Geneva

both a secular and church government which Knox regarded
as well-nigh ideal.

John was eager to study the form of government which had
been established. He was equally desirous of having long conversations with the master on knotty questions of theology. If
God had foreordained whatsoever came to pass how could He
have left for men any freedom of will? How could one follow
the injunction of Saint Paul to "work out your own salvation
with fear and trembling?"

It was now getting cooler as darkness began to settle upon
the land. John looked about for a house or an inn where he
might spend the night. At a distance of perhaps a kilometer
ahead he espied a faint light which probably betokened a building of some kind, and he increased his pace.

He passed a broad field which a farmer had just begun to
plow and came on a wooded area where evergreen trees pressed
on the road from either side. He walked even faster, both because of his eagerness to arrive at the source of the light and
because the evening cold began to penetrate to his bones.

Suddenly, without warning, a group of men came out from
among the trees and set upon him. So sudden was the attack
that, when a club whirled through the air, he was felled by the
first blow. For a moment he was stunned but his thick cloak
protected him from serious damage.

With clubs the entire group now began their attack, raining
blows upon him from every direction. John's own stout staff
had been knocked from his hand but lay within easy reach.
When his head was partly cleared he reached for it, suddenly
sprang upright, and began whirling it about his head like a
windmill.

Some of his enemies' thrusts penetrated this defense but his
own blows had their effect upon his assailants for he bowled
them over like ninepins.

The battle was quickly concluded. Three of his assailants lay
in the road, the rest disappeared. He felt gingerly of the lumps
which his opponents had raised on his head. Then he turned his
attention to his groaning assailants. He assumed that they were
thieves from the countryside, but in the waning light he recognized one of them as an Englishman who had been in Cox's
company.

"Why did you attack me?" he asked the man. "I had done you
no harm."

A groan was the only reply.

One of the others sat up, shook his head to clear it, and then made reply. "You treated our leader scurvily, John Knox."

"Your leader?" Knox returned in amazement. "Did Richard Cox send you?"

"He did not," the man replied. "We came of our own will."

"But armed to do me harm?"

"We but wanted to make clear to you that you could not oppose Messer Cox with impunity. Whoever stands against him deserves what you received."

"But this is no way to convert those with whom you disagree."

"You have just concluded a sturdy effort thus to convert us," the man replied.

"I was not seeking to convert you," John Knox retorted. "I do not regard conversions by force as effective."

"Your efforts were," the man returned.

John helped him to his feet.

"See if your comrades can walk," John said. "Are they injured?"

"I think not," the man replied. "Thy stout club merely stunned them momentarily."

With John's aid the man helped the other two to their feet. The men looked about them groggily.

"Can you get back to your comrades?" John asked.

"We can make it," the man said.

John shook hands with his former assailants but felt that the situation called for a short sermon.

" 'Twas a cowardly act," he asserted, "to set upon one man as you did."

"Aye, that it was," one of them agreed. "We are sorry, Messer Knox. And we hope you bear us no ill will."

John laughed.

"No," he said, "I have naught against you. And I hope that you will forgive me for the argument that I used."

Ruefully the spokesman said, " 'Twas effective, Messer Knox. 'Twas powerfully effective."

"Then I shall bid you Godspeed and be on my way," Knox replied. "I hope we shall meet again under more pleasant circumstances."

"Only so would we wish to meet you again," one of the men retorted.

Despite his assorted bumps John felt good as he picked up his bundle of clothing and started on his way. The encounter had warmed his blood and it had somehow cheered him.

After traveling for a short distance he came upon the cottage in which he had seen the light. He went up to the door, rapped on it with his knuckles, and finally it was opened an inch by a man who was obviously a woodcutter from the worn leather breeches which encased his limbs.

In halting German John said, "I'm on my way to Switzerland. Could I have shelter for the night?"

The man noted the evidence of the struggle in which he had been engaged and looked him over suspiciously.

"I am not a robber," John assured him, "but I was set upon by a company of men in the wood back there. They left a few marks upon me before I was able to beat them off."

"Come in, come in," the man invited. "But this is a strange happening, indeed. There are no thieves in this region. At least, there have been none heretofore."

"They were not thieves," John explained. "They were fellow countrymen of mine who did not approve of my preaching. I am John Knox, until recently the preacher in the English congregation at Frankfurt."

The man's eyes lighted.

"Oh, Protestant, *nicht wahr*?"

"Aye."

"Well, you are welcome. I am a follower of Martin Luther myself."

John entered the low-ceilinged room. Evidently the man dwelt there alone for the housekeeping arrangements gave evidence of the lack of a feminine touch.

"I have not much," the man said, "but you are welcome to what I have. I was just making rabbit stew for my supper."

"I would not take the food out of your mouth."

"There is plenty and to spare," the man replied.

After dining on the stew John spent the night in the cottage, sleeping on a pile of straw in the corner of the single room. The cottage was warm and John relaxed comfortably. He arose the next morning greatly refreshed. The woodcutter insisted on preparing a lunch for him to eat along the way before he would bid him Godspeed.

When John arrived in Geneva he discovered that John Calvin was busier than ever. Calvin had been successful in his bid to establish both a city government and a form of church government which were inextricably interwoven. In fact, John noted that Calvin had become something of a dictator in the realms both of church and state, albeit a benevolent and honest ruler.

Calvin had taken advantage of his powers, too, to persecute unbelievers, although he was exceedingly tolerant of Protestants who belonged to other sects than his own. He had envisioned a Geneva in which Protestants of all persuasions might worship God according to their own lights. Some of his Swiss friends were opposed to this program and wanted citizenship in the city to be reserved solely for the Swiss but he insisted that citizenship be granted all Protestants who had sought refuge in the city.

When John reported to Calvin what had happened in Frankfurt Calvin agreed that he had done the only thing possible under the circumstances.

"And you have arrived here at a most fortuitous time," he said. "Some of your countrymen and a group of English Protestants have settled amongst us. They have been worshiping with us but they should have their own services in the English tongue. I should like to appoint you to serve as their preacher."

"I would be happy to do so," John agreed, adding with a smile, "provided that there are no Richard Coxes among them."

"Richard Cox would have short shrift in Geneva," Calvin replied drily.

Calvin appointed a place where the English colony might worship and left the details of notifying the potential members of his congregation up to Knox. For the rest of the week the latter set about gathering his flock together and on Sunday he was greeted by almost one hundred expatriates.

These were a like-minded group who had chosen Geneva as their place of refuge in view of the fact that they accepted with very little question the teachings of Calvin as the basis for their theology and church government. The matter of the prayer book which had so agitated the church in England and had divided the congregations in Dieppe and Frankfurt was of little importance to them.

John was, therefore, able to follow his bent for preaching sermons on Biblical themes. He spent long hours in studying both the Old and New Testaments, finding riches in the Scriptures which he had not had opportunity to explore before.

He also became a pastor as he had been in Dieppe for a short time, visiting in the homes of members of his flock. The bracing air of the Swiss city brought a bloom to his cheeks and gave spring to his steps.

Calvin had more free time to spend in conference with him also and the two spent long hours together. They were opposites in temperament but each learned to appreciate the character and qualities of the other. Knox discovered that, for all his apparent placidity, John Calvin was a man of strong convictions and he clung to his convictions despite all obstacles.

But, differing from Knox, Calvin was content to bring about the changes which he saw were necessary by slow degrees. That Calvin's method was effective was evident from the character of the government which had been established both in the church and in the city. It was evident in the character of the citizens of the city, the quality of their lives, their earnest piety. It was especially evident on Sunday mornings when people flocked into the churches.

The few months that he was to remain in Geneva constituted for John a time of recapitulation of his life, a time of spiritual preparation for that which was to follow.

Near the end of the summer Calvin showed John a letter which he had just received from Scotland.

"Conditions are not ideal in your homeland," Calvin told him, "but your old friends believe that if you would now return you could provide the spark which might bring about a great reformation. The regent is still obdurate in her treatment of Protestants but the very excesses of which she has been guilty have stiffened the back of the opposition to her reign; and the young queen may soon be old enough to assume the throne for herself.

"Among those who are particularly eager that you should return is your old friend, Sir James Balfour. Would you consider returning at this time to Scotland to take part in the great events which seem to be in the making?"

"What think you, Messer Calvin?" John asked. "I have been most happy here with the congregation to which I have been ministering."

"And they have been exceedingly happy with your ministry," Calvin added. "Many of your people have thanked me for recommending your engagement as their minister."

"In view of that fact think you that I should now leave them after so short a time?" Knox inquired.

" 'Twould be well to pray over the matter," Calvin replied.

"Think on it, Brother John, and let me have your answer soon so that I may communicate it to our brethren in Scotland."

Knox was in much of a quandary. The peace and good will of Geneva appealed to him as a safe haven in a stormy sea of controversy. He was now in his forties and he had a natural yearning to get out of the storm. His life in a monastery had been a period of quiet. It had brought him his share of doubts and questions but little physical hardship. However, from the time that he had plunged into the Reformation movement he had been in the grip of a hurricane.

Now he was in a snug harbor, protected from the storms which were still raging about him. But is a sailor justified in holding his ship in port merely because storms may break at sea?

He was pondering these questions when he received a letter from Dame Elizabeth Bowes which seemed an answer to his prayers and questions.

For some considerable time he had been addressing her in his letters as "Dear Mother." Actually he corresponded more frequently with Dame Elizabeth than with Marjory. In some measure this had been due to his lack of ease in the role of a lover but it had also been a matter of expediency. Marjory would be able to see and read letters addressed to her mother but letters addressed to Marjory might be intercepted by Richard Bowes.

Richard was apparently not at all suspicious of the letters which his wife received. To be sure, she carried on a voluminous correspondence with leaders of the Reformation movement — and Richard decidedly did not approve of them — but he made no attempt to censor her letters. And he evidently was unaware of the fact that his wife was serving, in effect, as an intermediary between his daughter and John Knox.

Actually when Dame Elizabeth wrote to John it was as to a son although she still poured out her personal problems to him as to a father confessor. John assumed that the letter which he had received would be one of that nature. He was reluctant to open it for that reason, because of the intimate questions which Dame Elizabeth might ask, but eager to begin its perusal for the news which she might send regarding Marjory.

Finally, shrugging his shoulders, he slit open the envelope and took out the enclosed missive and began to read.

Dear son,

I have to inform you of the death of my beloved husband, Richard. His passing is a sore loss to me and to our family for, despite the many differences of opinion which we had, I loved him dearly. He was suddenly seized upon by a stroke and died peacefully a few hours later.

We are desolated by our loss and we walk about our familiar home constantly feeling his presence and sensing his nearness. The children especially miss him and his correction of their many faults and shortcomings.

Ne'ertheless, it may be that God, in His infinite wisdom, has seen fit at this time to take Richard home unto Himself in order that Marjory may now join you and you may be married. Sir Robert will, of course, attempt to deny the banns but we need not be too much concerned about his opposition for we see little of him.

We should wait a decent interval before you and Marjory are joined in marriage — out of respect to our departed husband and his wishes—but in the light of your own eagerness, in which Marjory joins, I believe that we could limit our mourning to a matter of two or three months.

We shall, therefore, await word from you concerning a time which would be most suitable for your marriage and the plans which you may devise for the wedding. We should like to have Marjory married to you here in Berwick but I am convinced that, with Mary on the throne, such would not be advisable. And I would be eager to be present for the nuptials but, in view of the long journey which would be necessary, I fear that Marjory will have to join you alone. Perhaps, however, you could go to Dieppe and be married there. In that case Marjory would not be confronted with the long journey from Dieppe to Geneva by herself.

Both Marjory and I will eagerly await word from you.

Thine own mother,
Elizabeth

The letter decided the matter for John. He would go to Scotland. It seemed a clear indication of the intervention of Providence and that there was a clear call for him to return to his native land. He shared this conviction with John Calvin.

"I am indeed glad for you, John," Calvin informed him. "If you should ever need to return to Geneva there will always be work here for you to do. But I am greatly concerned for the welfare of the church in Scotland and I feel that you are needed there.

"Now you can return thence and be married in your own native land. She would not need to come to either Dieppe or Geneva. Doubtless you are right. This does seem to be the clear call of God for you to go to Scotland."

"Well, then, Messer Calvin, if I may make so bold as to suggest a successor for our church here in Geneva, may I recommend William Whittingham? He is still in Frankfurt but it is an unhappy situation, since Messer Cox has so changed the character of the church there that it is but a faint semblance of a truly reformed church."

"An excellent suggestion," Calvin agreed, "but it must, of course, be subject to the approval of the membership of your church. Since we believe that authority stems from the people they must be consulted and the choice must be freely theirs."

"I feel confident that they will approve," Knox assured him.

John immediately sat down to write the letters which would set in motion all of the procedures necessary. He addressed a missive to Mrs. Bowes and another to Marjory. He had not previously written Marjory directly and he still felt that it would be advisable to include Marjory's letter in the same envelope which contained the one to her mother, for he suspected that Sir Robert might continue the surveillance which Marjory's father had initiated. He addressed another letter to Sir James Balfour asking him to make the necessary arrangements for a wedding in Edinburgh. He wrote William Whittingham to inquire if he would be willing to consider the pastorate of the church in Geneva in the event that the congregation were favorable to calling him. He painted for him a rosy picture of the character of the membership of the church.

He called the leaders of the Geneva church together and told them of his conversations with Calvin and of his decision to return to Scotland.

Douglas Mackenzie, who had been a professor in the University of Glasgow before he had fled Scotland, moved for the release of John Knox from his pastoral duties "at his convenience."

" 'Tis not because we long to see ye go," he explained, "but for the sake of Scotland. I, too, agree that ye are needed there. And if this man Whittingham is all that ye say he is — and I trust y'r judgment implicitly — I think we should invite him to come and serve here."

The others agreed.

But one of the Englishmen insisted that a condition be imposed. "Always providing," he suggested, "that the way shall be left open for you to return to the church here. Even if we engage Whittingham the church is large enough to support the two of you, and there would be plenty of work for the two of you."

"And we would want also to support the wife that he will marry," added Mackenzie cannily.

The members of the church council nodded their heads in approval.

"And the family which we hope that he will have," appended the Englishman with a smile.

"I am not even married yet, and ye have me with a house full of bairns," Knox retorted.

"They will come on apace," Mackenzie sagely remarked.

Out of their meager personal resources the church people raised a considerable sum of money which they presented to John Knox.

Mackenzie was their spokesman. " 'Tis not proper that a man should take a wife without a groat in his purse," he said. "We would that ye should have a proper marriage when you get to Edinburgh."

John had little hope that the letter which he had written to James Balfour would be delivered. He had not heard from him for some time except through Calvin and he had no news as to the location of his friend, but within two months he received an answer. Balfour was in Edinburgh where, he said, there were a considerable number of people who were secretly meeting in small groups.

"The flame is burning brightly," he wrote. "It has never died out, and we shall welcome your presence among us."

He promised to make arrangements for the forthcoming nuptials of John and Marjory.

" 'Twould be just as well to have the wedding in Edinburgh," he wrote. "To be sure, there is no safe place for Protestants in any part of Scotland, but we are as secure here as anywhere. And conditions in England are much worse. The queen has inundated the land with the blood of martyrs. No one in her realm is safe anywhere.

"It is said that even her Spanish husband has remonstrated with her and urged moderation. But the woman is a vampire. The more blood she spills the more insatiable her lust for further killings."

Upon receipt of a letter from Dame Elizabeth John set out for Scotland. Mrs. Bowes promised John that as soon after his arrival in Scotland as he desired she and Marjory would join him for the wedding.

12

John decided that it would be the part of wisdom to assume some guise other than that of a scholar when he landed on the Scotch coast. During his years in the monastery he had become quite proficient as a carpenter and it was as a carpenter, therefore, that he reached Edinburgh.

He reasoned with himself that, as a disciple of the Carpenter of Nazareth, it surely was not wrong to appear in Scotland as one who followed that trade.

He had anticipated that Scotland would be in turmoil as was England but there were no evidences of strife as he walked the streets of the city. No one recognized him. No one gave him more than a cursory glance. It seemed strange to hear once more the Scotch tongue. He had had Scotsmen in the church at Berwick, others at Frankfurt and in Geneva, but they had been minority groups and most of them had been university men whose mode of speech differed little from that of their English cousins.

It was good to hear once more the Scotch tongue as it was spoken by tradesmen and artisans, the language of the street and countryside, and particularly the speech of the lowlands.

If there were any changes in the city itself he did not notice them. Holyrood Palace seemed as grimy as ever, St. Giles cathedral as weather-worn as he remembered it of yore. The sights and the smells were as always. But it was good to be *hame* once more — and Scotland was home to John.

He decided to make his first call on a schoolmaster, Ian McBeath, who, as he recalled, was one of the active participants in the Reformation movement. If he lived in the same house which he had occupied before John would not have to make inquiry concerning his residence and he sensed that the fewer questions that he had to ask the better it would be. Sir James Balfour had either forgotten to tell him where he was lodging or had decided not to commit his address to paper should the letter that he had written fall into the hands of his enemies.

But McBeath would know where Sir James was living if any-one would. Hence, he found his way into the old town within the walls of the city and sought out the house which he had occupied when John had last seen him.

At first he did not recognize the old man who answered the knock on the door and then he realized that it must be McBeath himself.

The man peered at him, a puzzled frown on his face.

"Thy face is somehow familiar," he remarked, scanning John's features.

"You are Ian McBeath, are you not?" John inquired.

"The same," Ian replied, "and I am sure that I should know ye but I cannot now recall thy name. There is something about thy voice that brings back memories. But, fie upon me, I have not invited thee to enter."

John stepped over the threshold and preceded his host into the simply furnished little room.

"But I remember you well, Ian McBeath," John said, "and I recall your fine leadership in the Reformation movement."

The man surveyed him with an uneasy glance.

"Aye," he acknowledged, "but we do not speak of the Reformation as casually as you do. We have found it wise to exercise caution — more caution by far than was necessary some few years ago."

"You need no caution in speaking to me," John remarked with a smile. "I am John Knox."

The man's face lighted.

"John Knox," he exclaimed incredulously. "It is many years since I heard you preach in the parish kirk at St. Andrews. Mon, I had thought thee dead many years agone."

"Aye," John replied. "In truth I should have died but the good Lord preserved me, and has finally directed my footsteps back to my homeland and to your door."

"And you are thrice welcome here. But come, mon, what do you now in Scotland?"

"I come back to begin preaching once more. Our friends in the Free Kirk urged me to return from Geneva where I have been with Calvin."

"With Calvin, indeed. We have heard much concerning that brilliant mon."

"And I come bearing his greetings to the church and his promise of every assistance that he can render us," John explained.

"Ye're sore needed, I can tell you," said McBeath.

John wanted to add that he had also come to Scotland to be wed but decided that such was a personal matter in which McBeath would be little interested.

"I have come seeking Sir James Balfour, too. We were both prisoners, chained to the oars of a French galley," John explained further. "Do you ken where he is?"

"Aye," McBeath acknowledged, "but 'tis a closely guarded secret. The regent would like to lay him by the heels if she could but, in truth, I do not think that the crown is seeking him with much diligence. At the moment the regent seems to be willing to let sleeping dogs lie, and Sir James is one of those."

McBeath agreed to take John to the temporary residence of Sir James but advised waiting until nightfall.

"We had best go armed when we seek him out," McBeath explained. " 'Twould not be wise to go in daytime, but it's dangerous to be abroad in the city at night without a sword."

Thus girded and accompanied by two other stout fellows who were similarly accoutered, they walked down dark streets, staying close together, and although they encountered suspicious-looking characters, they came to the house on the outskirts of the city where Sir James was quartered.

John immediately noted the change in Sir James' appearance. There were lines deeply etched in his face which had not been there when they parted in Berwick, but Sir James was overjoyed to meet him.

"I have longed to see thee for many months," he said, "and now are my hopes fulfilled. We have sore needed you here in Scotland and the time is ripe for your preaching once more."

"In St. Andrews?" John asked.

"Aye. I remember when we passed the castle that you said some day you would preach there again. That time may not be too far off. The Reformation is now being espoused by the nobles," Sir James asserted. "Doubtless this is due in part to their detestation of the regent and her French advisers but, whatever their motives, they are now on the side of the Reformation as they were not before."

"But first I must be married," John reminded him.

"Agreed," Sir James remarked decisively. "We'll write Dame Elizabeth advising her of your presence and bidding her come with all haste."

"Where shall we be married?"

"Where but in Edinburgh?" Sir James retorted.

"It can be arranged?"

"It is arranged. Sir Douglas Mackenzie will have the wedding in the great hall of his castle. You will stay with him until the Bowes come from England and they, too, will be quartered there."

"But will they be safe? He is well known and surely word regarding the wedding would get around the city," Knox remarked.

" 'Twill be done in secret. His servants are all Protestant, and he himself is too powerful for the regent to dare to provoke him, but it is arranged that the wedding shall be so quietly conducted that none shall know of it aside from the few whom you desire to have present."

"Have you arranged for a minister?"

"Yes, indeed, subject to your approval. Duncan Campbell who was, like yourself, formerly a priest and has since married also, will perform the rites. There'll be no mass in connection with it, I can assure you."

"I shall never cease to be grateful to you for all of these services, Jamie," Knox remarked, giving his arm a friendly squeeze. "You've been more than a brother to me."

The early frosts had painted the leaves in shades of red, yellow and orange when Marjory and her mother arrived in Edinburgh. John had suggested that they come by coach, timing their arrival so that it would be after nightfall, if that would be possible. Despite Sir James' assurance that the queen regent would not interfere he thought it best to cloak their arrival with all possible secrecy.

John had been busy with his writing when he heard the clatter in the courtyard. He glanced out of the window of his study and saw the two ladies being helped from the coach. He hurried down the staircase and out into the yard.

He first embraced Dame Elizabeth since it was she who flew to his arms.

"My son! My son!" she exclaimed, and then tears streamed down her face. "I have so longed to see you, have so eagerly yearned for your comfort and your good counsel."

"It is a joy to see you, Mother," he murmured. "It was good of you to come with Marjory."

"I could not let you be married without being present," she replied.

"To be sure. To be sure."

She clung to him, beginning to tell him the story of Richard's last days of life.

"But Marjory . . ." John murmured, attempting to disengage himself.

"Yes, indeed, she has come, too," Dame Elizabeth remarked, still clinging to him.

"I . . ." John began.

"You will have time for her when I have told you all," Dame Elizabeth said severely.

"Nay, Mother. Thy story will take over long. Tell it me later," John replied, freeing himself from her embrace.

Immediately he gathered Marjory into his arms.

"Dearly beloved," he whispered while she buried her face in the hollow of his shoulder.

He held her thus for what seemed an eternity and then whispered, "Long ago thou didst command me to kiss thee. Command me again."

She looked up at him shyly.

"But there are so many people . . ." she murmured.

She did not have a chance to finish.

"They all expect it," John returned, boldly kissing her on the lips.

Dame Elizabeth laid hold of John's arm, interrupting the tender scene.

"Richard was so sweet towards the end," she remarked to him, "so kind and considerate. He warned Marjory that she should not marry you but he said that if she did he would forgive you and her. I must tell you about his last words."

"Later, Mother, later," said John patiently. He added in a whisper for Marjory's ear, "If we go into the house we can find a quiet spot where we can talk."

There was, however, to be no private conference at the moment. Sir Douglas and his lady had to be introduced and they greeted their guests warmly. But the awkwardness of the first moments were over and they all trooped into the great hall.

Although they had dined earlier Lady Mackenzie ordered a meal prepared for the guests in which all joined. The meal was a merry one. Sir Douglas remarked on the beauty of the bride-to-be, bringing becoming blushes to the cheeks of Marjory. John's cup of joy was brimmed to overflowing.

The wedding of Marjory Bowes and John Knox was a quiet

one. Present were only a few of the leaders of the Reformation movement, the minister, James Balfour, McBeath, and the Mackenzies.

After Duncan Campbell had pronounced the two man and wife Dame Elizabeth was the first to kiss John. She shoved her daughter aside and bussed him heartily on the lips. John was overcome with surprise but suffered his mother-in-law to do her will. Yet he was frankly disappointed, for he had looked forward with keen anticipation to the nuptial kiss.

When he was able to disengage himself from Dame Elizabeth the tender embrace of his bride was something of an anti-climax but the two clung to one another for a long minute before turning to receive the felicitations of their friends.

"Ye'll be more of a man than ever, John Knox," James Balfour remarked.

"She'll be my strong right arm," John replied.

John felt that he had never in all of his life experienced such joy as that which now surged through his veins. He was a married man. He had new responsibilities, a new reason for living. But he also felt as if he had by his marriage acquired new powers. There had been times in the past when discouragements almost quelled his spirit. Now discouragements might come but they would be shared with Marjory.

All about him there was a bustle of talk. Everyone was speaking at once.

Dame Elizabeth came to him and threw her arms about him once more.

"If Richard could only have been here to have shared our joy!" she exclaimed in a shower of tears.

Marjory caught her words and whispered to her, "Bear in mind, Mother, that Father was opposed to our marriage from the start. We never could have been married this day if he had been living. Now let us just forget about him for a while."

"But, Marjory . . ." her mother wailed.

"I do mean it, Mother," Marjory said sharply. "I long ago forgave him his opposition. But let us not make a saint out of a stubborn sinner."

Her mother shook her head sadly. John decided that it was time for him to intervene.

"We forget our friends," he remarked. "Mother, won't you tell Messer McBeath about the situation in England? He is so keenly interested in the progress of the Reformation that I am certain he would like to know how matters are going in our neighboring country."

Mrs. Bowes brightened visibly.

"I should be delighted to do so," she agreed.

Espying McBeath, she made her way to his side.

"My dear son John wanted me to inform you concerning the state of our work in England," she remarked, gently leading McBeath to a secluded corner.

The latter flashed a quizzical look at John but obediently followed Mrs. Bowes. Soon they were absorbed in conversation.

Marjory gave John a merry smile.

"I perceive that thou art also a diplomat, John," she remarked, "a quality which I never expected to find in thee."

"Your mother is a wonderful woman, dear," he replied. "There is no truer advocate of the cause of Christ anywhere in these islands. It is only when she is launched on the story of her own problems and perplexities that she becomes tiresome."

"Indeed!" she remarked cryptically. "I had never thought to see you finally become aware of her failings."

"Remember," he replied, "that I have had to answer letters from her over a period of many years. I regard her with sincere affection, but because of my warm feeling for her I can also understand her. I know her need for a sympathetic ear and that Ian McBeath hath."

For a short time John Knox, his bride and Mrs. Bowes were guests of the Mackenzies.

Mrs. Bowes apparently had no intention of departing as John had expected and he mentioned the matter to his wife.

"Oh, Mother intends to live with us," she remarked airily.

"But what about the children?" John asked in dismay. "Will your brothers and sisters also join us?"

"Oh, no," Marjory said. "They have gone to live with my older brothers and sisters. I am very much afraid, John, that our dream of a life to be lived alone together is not to be."

"But," she added practically, "Mother is now in possession of the money from my father's estate and if she lives with us we shall not have to worry about paying the green-grocer for our food."

John shrugged his shoulders.

Dame Elizabeth was a host in herself as an advocate of the reformed church. If so be that she intended to be domiciled with them she would be of genuine assistance. If only she would not plague him with the problems which related to the condition of her soul!

John had made no preparations for a domicile for his bride. He was actually not too well aware that marriage entailed such responsibilities.

Sir James Balfour remarked to Sir Douglas Mackenzie, "We must make some provision for Messer Knox. I am convinced that marriage is what was needed to bring out the best in the man but we cannot expect him to live in the same fashion as he did before he was married."

"And I understand that his mother-in-law intends to stay with the couple," Sir Douglas remarked.

"A remarkable woman," Sir James said, "but somewhat of a problem!"

"That is a most charitable characterization of the female," Sir Douglas added drily.

"Can we find a house for him and his women?" Sir James inquired. "Do you know of any that are available?"

"They are welcome to stay with us," Sir Douglas said.

"Nay. 'Twould not be fair to you and 'twould not be the right thing for John."

"Well, then, we do have a house within the courtyard in which they could live by themselves but they would be protected by our own servants. And John may soon become the target of the opposition of the queen regent and her party."

"Would she not transfer her opposition to you?" Sir James inquired.

"She and her henchmen already have me written down in their bad books," Sir Douglas retorted. "I could not become more objectionable to her by doing so."

" 'Tis most generous of you, Sir Douglas," Sir James murmured.

For a short time the Knoxes and Mrs. Bowes remained in the Mackenzie home but Marjory and John were eager to settle down by themselves although John was not too pleased at the thought of Dame Elizabeth living with them.

Yet the arrangement worked out better than he had anticipated and, since he felt that he had to accept the invitations to preach and to lecture which came in from all parts of Scotland, he resigned himself to the idea of having his mother-in-law live with them.

Since John had never had to concern himself about the matter of food and shelter, clothing and the practical necessities of life, it was perhaps just as well that Dame Elizabeth was domiciled with them in view of the fact that her husband had made ample provision for her. Thus, neither John nor Marjory ever had to worry about their food, fuel or clothing.

John felt some considerable unease at the thought of Dame Elizabeth's leaving her children in England but Marjory assured him that the arrangement was an eminently practical one. "The children often spent some time with my older brothers and sisters," she explained. "Remember that there were fifteen of us. I'm not sure that Mother was always able to remember our names."

"I'd like to be the father of fifteen," John remarked wistfully, "but I believe that we had better stop far short of that mark."

"Most assuredly we should," Marjory agreed.

They were happy in the little home which the Mackenzies made available to them. Dame Elizabeth had been accustomed to a considerable number of servants but she was an exceedingly capable housekeeper. In her efficient way she took charge of such arrangements in the Knox home. Marjory would have preferred to do the work herself but John pointed out to her that if they allowed Dame Elizabeth to take charge it would keep her occupied and happy.

"To be sure, despite your assurances, I feel guilty about thy younger brothers and sisters," he told her. "They should have their mother's care and affection."

"Be not concerned about that," Marjory replied. "They are well cared for by my older sisters and brothers, and mother has made ample allowance for their keep."

Having settled the matter of family living, John plunged into his work for the movement. Scotland was in a sorry situation. The hope for the country lay in the nobility but the various clan leaders were so occupied with petty disputes among themselves that they had little time for the major ills which faced the land.

The queen regent was disposed to permit any measure of religious freedom which would be necessary to keep the peace. She had determined that she would eventually turn over to her daughter the scepter of a united realm. Her major concern was to keep strong ties with France and embarrass England as much as possible without coming to the brink of war.

The bishops warned her against John Knox but she was not disposed to take action against him if she would thereby alienate the support of some of the nobility.

John himself was no longer concerned merely to protest against the practices of the Roman Church. Having observed the reforms which Calvin had instituted in Geneva and which Cranmer had begun in England, he was determined that Scotland should have a reformed church which would sound a positive note, and his preaching began to mirror his thinking.

The opportunity to sound such a note came in November. John Erskine invited him to visit him at Dun which was just a few miles inland from Montrose where Wishart had held his classes in Greek.

"I shall invite a group of northern leaders to hear you if you will come," Erskine wrote. "And if Sir James Balfour is not otherwise occupied persuade him to come with you if you can. He has suffered so much for the cause that he, too, would have a profound influence upon these men."

John accepted Erskine's invitation and he and Sir James met daily with the company in the large home which was almost a castle. Among those who assembled there were rugged Scottish lairds, each with a few of his chosen retainers. Many of the men had been feuding with other members of the group but they forgot their differences as they met daily. Possibly the prayers of Knox and Balfour had more to do with accomplishing this end than their daily messages.

John's messages also assumed a nationalistic tone. He pointed out to the Scots that they were, in effect, but vassals of France politically and in their religion they were vassals of Rome. To be a free nation and to have a free religion they would have to break the ties which bound them to both foreign powers. To John's way of thinking the tie with Rome was the more dangerous. If that could be broken they could be free of France much more quickly.

His thinking appealed to the leaders who were present. They were swayed by his eloquence and also by the practical note which was sounded by James Balfour who had a special appeal for them in view of the fact that he was not of the clergy.

From Dun John and Sir James went south into Lothian where another group of nobles assembled. Among those who heard him frequently were two future regents of Scotland, the

Earl of Moray and the Earl of Mar. At the moment the Earl of Mar was governor of Edinburgh castle.

Although the capital was close by his preaching points, apparently news of his preaching did not reach the palace, for if John had preached in Edinburgh as he did in the little town of Calder close by he would have been arrested and brought to trial for treason immediately, but the queen regent and her advisers were apparently little concerned with what happened in the areas which they considered the provinces. If all was quiet in the city and the nobles did not stir up trouble there apparently was little danger for her and the realm.

Following this mission John returned to Edinburgh for a short rest.

"Would that you did not have to be away so often," Marjory plaintively remarked to him. "I feel a need of thee."

"Oh, my love, I would that I did not need to be away at all but that is my mission in life. It is my responsibility."

"And do you have no responsibility for your family?" she inquired tartly.

He smiled.

"But we have no family as yet, beloved. My only responsibility is for you and your dear mother — and the two of you can manage well and are perfectly secured within the walls of Sir Douglas' castle."

"You will one day have a family," Marjory retorted, "and we should prepare for it."

"Time enough for that when we have our first bairn," he replied.

"Aye," she answered dutifully.

13

John seriously endeavored to spend more time in Edinburgh but the requests for his services came so frequently that he felt he could not refuse them. Wherever he went he received a warm welcome. His hosts for the most part were Scottish nobles.

By Easter of 1556 the atmosphere had changed so much that he felt free to preach openly. He revisited the areas where he had been speaking and great throngs of people came to hear him.

So emboldened did he become that the news of his activities reached the ears of the queen regent once more, this time with the strong protests of the Scottish bishops. If Mary did not sense the danger which Knox presented the bishops did. When she was disposed to make light of the influence of his preaching they reminded her that his stirring messages in the parish kirk at St. Andrews had lighted a fire which had never burned out.

"Your grace had best remember that, for all his appearance, he is a flame in the pulpit. He is thunder and lightning, and one of his thunderbolts might well topple the throne," one of them bluntly cautioned.

She agreed, therefore, that it might be advisable to lay him by the heels. But, mindful of the Biblical incident in which Pilate, at the instance of the Jewish priests, was compelled to exercise judgment over a man who was accused of treason against Rome, one Jesus of Nazareth, she decided that she would let the bishops pull their own chestnuts out of the fire. If Knox were to be brought to trial they would be the responsible parties — not she.

She did grant them permission to conduct such a trial. This was all that they required. They summoned him to appear in Edinburgh for trial.

Knox read the order for his appearance to Sir James and Sir Douglas.

"Messer John Knox," the summons began, "by order of her majesty, the queen regent, you are hereby commanded to appear before a council to be convened in the Church of the Blackfriars on the fifteenth of May next to answer to various charges which have been laid against you:

"To wit, that you have sought in your preaching to undermine the authority of God's duly consecrated bishops, and

"Furthermore, that you are substituting for the Eucharist wholly alien and wrongful forms of celebration of the same, and

"Furthermore, that you are critical of the Holy Church itself and thereby seek to inspire rebellion against her.

"Therefore, you are instructed to appear before the council at the time and place specified to make answer to these charges."

John finished the reading and looked expectantly at his two friends.

"I wouldn't go," Sir James bluntly advised. "You will recall what happened to Jan Huss when he came before the church council in Prague. The bishops are sufficiently wroth with you to take your life."

"I cannot well avoid such a trial," Knox returned. "If I should fail to appear they could condemn me and thereafter I would be a fugitive."

"You could return to Geneva," Sir James suggested.

"I would not be forever running away," Knox replied.

"It is not running away," Sir James objected. "John Calvin has indicated that your presence in Geneva is greatly to be desired by him and his council."

"Nay, Sir James, John Knox is right," Sir Douglas interposed. " 'Twould seem to many as if he were a-feared of the bishops if he did not appear."

"Have you ever been confined in a dungeon, my friend?" Sir James asked quietly. "Do you know what it is to have your bed overrun with rats? I do not want John to suffer confinement again and with the court already making its decision in advance that is what would happen."

Sir Douglas smiled.

"I do not want John to be laid by his heels either, especially since he has but so recently taken unto himself a bride. But I promise you that he will not be arrested. Instead, we shall build a fire under the bishops that should warm them up."

"And how would you do that?"

"By having John present himself at Blackfriars, at the same time that we send with him such a company of his supporters as will give pause to the proceedings of the trial."

"There is not much time."

"There is enough," Sir Douglas replied laconically. "But that is a matter which concerns us. I shall speak to my friends. You will speak to yours. Tell them what is in the wind."

"You would not have them come armed?" Sir James inquired.

"No, not at all," Sir Douglas replied. "There would be no need. The bishops cannot intimidate the nobles of Scotland, I care not how many of them attend or what is the force at their backs."

On May fifteenth John Knox entered the Church of the Blackfriars by the principal door. He had decided that he would make his entry alone while his friends remained on the steps.

"Let me but stand outside that I may see when it would be best to have your friends follow you," Sir James suggested.

"You may do that if you will," John agreed, "but wait until I give the word to enter."

Sir James approved the plan.

As John stepped into the church he was confronted by a solid phalanx of bishops. They stared stonily at him as if by their very glances they would intimidate him. There was a hushed whispering. John caught a few of the words . . . "Didn't think he'd dare to come" . . . "the heretic in person" . . . "considers himself to be above the bishops" . . . "consorted with that heretic, Calvin . . ."

He knew then beyond a doubt that, although there were some of the clergy in Scotland who had enlisted in the Reformation movement, the leadership of the church was still obedient to Rome.

He turned about, therefore, before stepping forward and nodded to Sir James. Sir James stepped outside and nodded to Sir Douglas.

"They're like a pack of wolves — and they think that they have a sheep all to themselves," he remarked.

"Good. We'll be the dogs who guard the sheep," Sir Douglas replied. He nodded to the men who were waiting and they walked into the church.

As an indication of where they stood on the issues before the court the nobles ranged themselves alongside and back of John Knox. It was all done so unostentatiously that it seemed a ghostly company which, grim-faced, stood back of John.

The bishops had been equally stern-visaged when John walked in alone. Now mouths sagged and their glances turned away.

John was the first to break the deep silence which prevailed.

"May it please your excellencies, I have appeared in answer to a summons which I received and to reply to the charges contained in said summons. I am ready to answer to these charges."

His words were received in silence.

One bishop looked to another. No one apparently wanted to speak.

"The order stated that the council was convened by authority of her majesty, the queen regent. May I inquire if her majesty is represented here?"

There was no answer to this question.

Finally one of the men seated at the table spoke up. John did not recognize him but assumed that he was the spokesman.

"It is probably an exaggeration to speak of the matters which are before this council as charges, Messer Knox," he asserted mildly. "But some of us, knowing that you had been absent from Scotland for some time, during a part of which, we understand, you were a prisoner in a French galley, felt that we might counsel with you concerning those things which had happened during your absence.

"We felt that if you were aware of the direction which the church has taken in these latter years it might enable you the better to fit into the life of the church in Scotland."

He continued at some length, suggesting that reforms of various kinds were being instituted but failing to specify what these were. John heard the speaker out.

Finally, impatiently, he inquired, "There are no charges, then, against me?"

"No charges as such," the spokesman replied.

"But surely you expect me to make answer to the accusations which were contained in the summons," John asserted.

There was no answer but he heard them whispering among themselves. One strident voice insisted, "Don't let him speak. He'll but preach a long sermon."

Now from one of the nobles came the demand, "Let John Knox make answer."

There was a general shaking of heads among the ecclesiastics. The spokesman hastily said, "The meeting is over. There have been no charges against John Knox. No decision is reached. We have done."

There was now nothing to do but depart. But the fact that no specific accusations had been leveled against John left him free to preach in Edinburgh. This he began to do quite openly. To be sure, he was not invited to take the pulpit at St. Giles but there were smaller churches whose priests, although they had not yet openly espoused the cause of reformation, were willing to invite him to occupy their pulpits, and this he did.

His experience in Geneva began to tell in his preaching. For a long time he had been basically denunciatory in his messages. He realized now the necessity for sounding a positive note. He had been protestant. Now he became evangelical.

His sermons regarding the Lord's Supper no longer denounced the mass but, instead, emphasized the position that when Jesus instituted the supper he did so as a commemorative feast. He said, "This do in remembrance of me." And all who were present partook of both the bread and the wine. Knox invited his auditors to partake of both elements. He initiated the plan of distributing the elements to the people in their pews instead of having them come forward to the altar rail.

Many people came to hear him solely out of curiosity. He was a new sensation. He was a Scotsman who had preached acceptably in both England and on the continent. One of the curious was the Earl Marischal of Scotland, William Keith. At first he came only to the evening meetings and sat far to the rear in dimly lighted churches. Later he came openly and finally introduced himself to John and invited him to come to his home for a conference.

With Douglas Mackenzie and James Balfour John accepted the invitation.

After they had spoken casually for some time the earl inquired, "Were you aware, Messer Knox, that the queen regent intervened with the bishops before the trial to which you had been summoned took place?"

"I was not."

"Are you positive of this?" Sir James inquired cannily.

"Certain," Keith replied. "They could not halt it in time but they were not ready to lay charges against you."

"But why did she intervene?" John asked.

"Because she likes not the bishops. She senses that they exercise too much power," Keith replied.

"But she hath no fondness for me," John asserted simply.

"She is shrewd," Keith said. "Make no mistake about that. She would play you off against the bishops, the bishops against you. But it pleases her at the moment to act on your behalf. I have all this on excellent authority."

Keith was actually wrong, as John was to discover later, although he made his assertions in good faith. The queen regent had not acted in the matter at all. It is doubtful if she was even aware of the fact that John had been summoned for trial; possibly she did not even have word regarding it or knew what the outcome had been.

"It might be wise to capitalize on her opposition to the bishops at this time by addressing a letter to her majesty," Keith suggested.

"Would it carry weight with her?" Mackenzie asked.

"If it pleased her fancy and she thought that it might strengthen her hold on the government it surely would," Keith replied.

"It could do no harm to try," Balfour suggested.

"Do ye know Alexander Cunningham, the Earl of Glencairn?" Keith inquired.

"I do indeed," Balfour replied.

"He has a somewhat tarnished reputation," Keith returned, "but he is heart and soul in the reform. Yet he is also in favor with the court. If you should write such a letter to her majesty it is quite possible that he would present it to her. There is no one who would exert as much influence as he."

John decided that it would be advisable to have the assistance of Balfour and Mackenzie in the composition of the letter. He did not mistrust his own literary powers but he wanted to indite an epistle which would appeal to her majesty. Therefore, shortly after he had received the suggestion, the three set about composing the message.

John had written the first paragraph before they met.

He read it to his two friends. "Superfluous and foolish it may appear to many that I, a man of base estate and condition, dare enterprise to admonish a princess so honorable, endowed with such singular grace and wisdom. I doubt not but the rumors which came to your grace's ears concerning me have been such, that if all reports were true, I would be unworthy to live on the earth. I have been traduced as an heretic, accused as a false teacher and seducer of the people, in addition to other charges which might easily kindle the wrath of magistrates who did not know that I was innocent of them."

Sir Douglas nodded his head affirmatively.

"Good," he said.

John went on. "Blessed be God, the Father of our Lord Jesus Christ, who by the dew of His heavenly grace, hath so quenched the fire of displeasure in your grace's heart that I have made bold to address you."

"Think you not that such may be a wee bit strong?" Sir James inquired. He paused for a moment and then added, "Nay, it may not be. Go on."

John continued. He was glad to hear that the queen regent was eager to affirm the authority of the crown and bring to Scotland a just and orderly rule. The morals of Scotland were in sore need of reformation and he was overjoyed to hear that she was concerned to develop in Scotland a sense of morality.

Then he dropped his bomb. "Ne'ertheless, vain is it to crave reformation in manners where the religion is corrupted. To be sure, it is dangerous indeed to attempt to bring about a reformation in religion but, as one appointed to reign over Scotland, I would admonish you as our lawful monarch to seek to bring it to pass."

"There you have come to the very heart of the matter," Sir Douglas remarked.

"Aye," agreed Sir James, "but John has led up to it deftly."

John Knox smiled.

"You would not say, 'daftly'?" he asked.

Sir James retorted, "Aye, we may all be daft for assuming that a letter will have any effect upon her majesty but it is barely possible that it will. You ken, o' course, what the good Saint Paul said about 'the foolishness of preaching.' Mayhap the foolishness of letter-writing may accomplish something after all."

John went on to inform the queen regent that the so-called "reformation" which many of her loyal subjects were seeking to bring to pass was not a new thing. It was an earnest attempt to bring the Church back to its earlier first century simplicity.

Her majesty also should beware of thinking that the care of religion was wholly a concern of the clergy; it was definitely a matter in which all magistrates should be vitally interested. Knox used the word "magistrates" to include all officers in secular government, particularly those with considerable authority. By this definition the queen and her counselors were "magistrates."

One thing the queen regent should avoid in her consideration of the validity of the reformation program. True religion was not to be judged by the number of voices espousing it, by customs, by the laws and determinations of men, nor by any other thing than the infallible dictates of inspired Scripture.

Knox wrote that while he was aware that a public reformation might be thought to exceed Mary's duty as regent, still she could not be bound to maintain idolatry and manifest abuses, nor to suffer the clergy to murder innocent men merely because they worshiped God according to His Word.

It was a strong letter. Sir James and Sir Douglas both conceded this. But they were united in their opinion that it was so courteously indited that her majesty could not fail to give it consideration.

"Moreover," Sir Douglas remarked, "she is now well versed in the English tongue. She will probably have a member of her court read the letter to her but she is able both to speak and read English. When she first came here she knew few words of our language but she has been here for some years now and she has been wise enough to know that if she would govern us she should speak the language which we use."

The letter concluded, the three presented it to the Earl of Glencairn. He read it carefully without comment, then reread it.

"What think you?" asked Douglas Mackenzie bluntly when he had finished. "Will her majesty respond to it?"

"'Tis well writ," Glencairn replied, "and of a certainty it is not a missive at which she could be offended. As to her attitude, I cannot say. I do know that there have been indications that she was inclined to favor the Reformation. When first she came to Scotland she was intensely loyal to the Church and if she had then received such a missive she would have clapped the writer into jail could she have laid hands upon him. But I believe that the situation has changed somewhat. Certainly it would do no harm to send it to her."

"But would you be willing to deliver it yourself?" asked Sir Douglas. "Neither Sir James nor I could present ourselves at court but you can do so, of course."

"I would have no hesitation whatsoever in presenting it," Glencairn replied.

The missive, therefore, was left in his hands. At the first opportunity he appeared before the queen regent.

"This letter which I bear was written by one of your majesty's loyal subjects," he said, "one John Knox, of whom your majesty has doubtless heard. He is a former priest but is now one of the leaders of the reformed party within the church."

This was not an altogether true evaluation of John's position but at the time the reformers in Scotland were still regarded as a group within the church.

The queen received the missive indifferently.

"We shall peruse it at our leisure," she remarked.

"But what answer shall I give to Messer Knox?" Glencairn inquired.

"The same as I have given you," she retorted sharply.

"Very well, your majesty," replied Glencairn, bowing and taking his leave.

The three who had been concerned with the composition of
the letter eagerly awaited his report.

"What answer did she give?" Sir James inquired.

"That she would read it at her leisure," Glencairn replied.

"She did not open it, then, while you were in her presence?"

"No."

"You did not urge her to do so?"

"If you knew her majesty you would know that such urging
would be the best way to assure that the missive would be consigned unopened to the flames," Glencairn explained.

"Think you that she will read it?" John inquired.

"I trust that she will," Glencairn replied, "but much will depend
upon what her mood is. She is a most capricious individual."

The queen actually did open the letter and had its contents
explained to her in French by one of her ladies-in-waiting.

She dismissed the epistle with an airy wave of her hand.

"Another subject who would tell me how to rule," she remarked.

While the letter was still before her the archbishop of Glasgow
was announced and bidden enter.

They conversed for a short time and then the queen regent
remembered the letter. She handed it to him with the remark,
"Please you, my lord, to read a *pasquil**."

If the queen considered the letter of no consequence the archbishop, however, did not. He soon shared its contents with other
bishops.

"We must see to it that nowhere — not in any church in Scotland — does John Knox receive a hearing," he said. "Close all
of your churches to him. Threaten with excommunication any
who permit him to lecture in their homes or in public places.
This renegade priest is not to be treated lightly."

John immediately felt the impact of the archbishop's order.
Invitations which had come to him were withdrawn without explanation. In the meantime he waited in vain for an answer
from the queen. Glencairn made discreet inquiries and discovered what had happened to the letter.

He told John what he had learned.

"She termed it a *pasquil*," he said.

"Do you think that she read it?" John asked.

"Doubtless she did," Glencairn returned, "but — what is more

* a silly note.

important — the archbishop of Glasgow also saw it. The clergy will be more than ever on their guard. It will be difficult for you to preach anywhere in Scotland from this time on."

"Think you that I should quit the country?"

"It might be well if you could absent yourself for a year or so,"

"I do not relish the thought of running away again but I have already discovered that word regarding the letter must have been noised abroad," John said, "for many doors which were open before are being closed again."

"It might be best for thee, then, to leave once more," Sir James suggested.

Only two days earlier John had received a letter from the church in Geneva inviting him to return and serve once more as pastor of the English flock there.

"Ye are sore needed," the letter read. "William Whittingham hath not thy preaching ability although he is a warmhearted and kindly man. He will serve with thee in all of the affairs of the church but he would have thee come and preach for us. The church has become apathetic and it should instead be the torchbearer of the entire reformed movement since we now have come to consider Geneva as the fountainhead of the Reformation."

He had been inclined to write and decline the invitation because of the urgency of service in Scotland but if all the doors which had been opened were to be closed to him then it might be advisable to return to Geneva. One other factor made the invitation most welcome. John Knox felt that Calvin was the true spokesman for the Reformation. For all of Knox's readiness to plunge into controversy and to defend his position he did not always feel that he had the facts to support his position. He felt intuitively that he was right but he knew that he needed logic and theology to back his stands.

John Calvin's clear thinking in the past had helped him to clear his own mind. It would be good to see the one whom he regarded with such veneration and esteem.

Knox, therefore, told his friends about the letter and his feelings in regard to it.

"Go, by all means," Sir Douglas advised him. "You will have no further opportunity for the present to preach in Edinburgh, and the doors are being closed against you all the way across the country. I would advise you to accept the invitation from Geneva."

"But it would seem as if I were running away again."

Sir James protested: "We know better than that. And we will inform you when it is advisable to return once more. But whenever doors are closed against you other doors open. For you to stay would not be doing our cause here in Scotland any real service. All that you would prove thereby is that you are a courageous man, and to those of us who know you that does not need to be proved."

"I shall go," John agreed, "but first I must journey to Castle Campbell for one more preaching engagement. The Earl of Argyle has bid me come to preach to some of his friends."

"Aye, he would invite you," replied Sir James, laughing. "The very fact that other doors have been closed against you would make him want to open the portals wide. He is a rebel of rebels."

"Would we had more like him," Sir Douglas exclaimed.

It was decided that John would send Marjory and Mrs. Bowes on to Dieppe where they could await him.

" 'Twill be safer that way," Sir James suggested. "They might attempt to detain you if all three of you left at the same time. And you have so many friends in Dieppe that your wife and Dame Elizabeth will be well cared for until you arrive."

Several evenings later Dame Elizabeth and Marjory left. They were put safely on board a ship and then John set out for Castle Campbell.

The Earl of Argyle was more than eighty years of age but a sturdy oak of a man who could spend the entire day hunting in the highlands or walking over his vast estate with apparently no evidences whatever of fatigue.

Castle Campbell was a rugged pile, craggy like its occupant. Life within the castle was equally austere. The wind whistled frigidly down winding corridors. Knox and the earl found in each other kindred spirits. The earl appreciated Knox's forthright manner of preaching. John found an appeal in Argyle's blunt mode of speech.

For several days services were held in the great hall of the castle. Men and often entire families rode in daily with their retainers. Soon the great hall would not contain them and John adjourned the meetings to the out-of-doors. A sunny slope on the south side of the castle was ideal for the purpose. John stood at the foot of the gentle decline and the people sat on the hillside.

"Ye must bide with us," Argyle curtly remarked when, after

two weeks of preaching, John announced that he would have to leave.

"But my family waits for me in Dieppe," John objected.

"Bring 'em back," Argyle commanded.

"I have written the church in Geneva accepting their call."

"Tell 'em ye have more important work in Scotland."

" 'Twould be a pleasant prospect," John admitted, "but I have promised and could not go back on my word."

"No, ye could not," Argyle acknowledged, "if ye've given y'r word."

Wistfully the earl added, "I had hopes that if ye stayed ye could do summat for my son Archibald. There is something lacking in him that I thought ye might supply."

"Each man must find it for himself," John told him. "Pray that he may."

"Aye, that I will," the earl said fervently.

In a very short time John took ship for Dieppe and rejoined his family. They were eager to be on their way to Geneva, having tarried over long in Dieppe and having a natural desire to see the beautiful city about which John had given them such glowing account.

14

John had scarcely arrived in Geneva when he received a summons from the ecclesiastical authorities in Edinburgh to appear for a second time before them. The bishops were well aware of the fact that Knox was out of the country but, since he failed to appear, they condemned him in absentia on the basis of the charges which had been originally lodged against him. Subsequently they burned him in effigy at the Mercat Cross, a well-known landmark in the city. Thus they disposed of a heretic and assumed that they would never hear from him again.

In the meantime he was busy in Geneva. Calvin was able to see him more often than on previous occasions and the friendship which had earlier developed between them ripened. Whittingham had returned to Frankfurt and, instead of this old colleague, he shared the pulpit of the church with an Englishman, Christopher Goodman. Preaching services were held frequently. During most of his ministry in Geneva John preached three times a week. Few of his sermons were less than two hours long.

In preparation for them he read the Old Testament in the original Hebrew and the New Testament in Greek. He had opportunity to discuss with the many scholars whom Calvin had attracted to Geneva the meaning of phrases which seemed to him obscure.

His congregation was small but warm and friendly. His preaching mellowed. None of his hearers needed to be converted to the Protestant cause. They represented various Protestant points of view and were quite free to express their differences of opinion with their preacher but all of the interchange was on the plane of frank and open discussion.

His feeling for Geneva was well expressed in a letter which he wrote to a friend whom he had made in London, a merchant by the name of William Locke. "In my heart," he said, "I could have wished, yea, and cannot cease to wish, that it might please God to guide and conduct yourself to this place, where, I neither fear nor am ashamed to say, is the most perfect school of Christ that ever was in the earth since the days of the apostles. In other places I confess Christ to be truly preached; but manners and religion to be so sincerely reformed, I have not yet seen in any other place beside."

John had many feminine correspondents also. These had evidently known something about his earlier correspondence with Mrs. Bowes for many letters came to him from women in both Edinburgh and London detailing their personal problems. John felt that whenever he received a letter an answer was necessary and he would write to them at considerable length in answer to their requests for advice.

Early in September of 1556 he began to sense a change in Marjory's attitude towards him. Earlier in their married life she had leaned upon him so completely, had soothed him when he was irritated, and had helped him relax when he was tense. The new Marjory seemed to be an altogether different person. She snapped at him over trifles and appeared worn and tired much of the time. The roses in her cheeks began to fade although the sunshine and climate of Geneva should have heightened her color.

"What aileth thy daughter?" he asked Mrs. Bowes one day.

"I try to please her and yet nothing that I do or say is approved
by her. And when I preached in other times she listened with
eagerness and interest. Now she turns her head away from me.
Her eyes, which were once so bright, now lack luster. Have I
offended her in any way, think you? Has she mentioned to you
aught which I may have done which does not meet with her
approval?"

"You do not know, then?" Mrs. Bowes said.

"Know what? Has something happened of which I am not
aware?"

"Nothing of which you should not be aware," she replied
with a smile.

"I do not understand."

Mrs. Bowes sniffed. "You do not understand!" she retorted.
"But, then, few men do. There is nothing wrong with Marjory
that time will not cure. After the baby is born she will be the
same as before."

"After the baby . . . no, you cannot mean that! You are telling
me that I am to be a . . . a father?"

"To be sure. Didst not know?"

"No. I was not aware . . . she said nothing to me . . . she
is all right?"

"She is in excellent health. The morning sickness, the languor,
the peculiar appetite, these are altogether normal with expectant
mothers."

"Oh, my wonderful Marjory!" John exclaimed in awe and
wonder.

Mrs. Bowes merely shrugged her shoulders.

"Not especially wonderful," she remarked. "It happens to all
women. It happened to me fifteen times."

"But this is the first time for Marjory. It has never occurred
before."

"No, but it will again," Mrs. Bowes retorted.

That evening, when he and Marjory were alone in their room,
he held her closely in his arms. Her response to the embrace
was passive. She allowed him to kiss her but there was no answer to the communication of love.

"Why did you not tell me, beloved?" he whispered. "I thought
you had grown cold to me."

"Tell you what?" she snapped.

"Tell me that you were to become a mother," he replied.

"Oh, that!" she exclaimed. "I thought you knew."

"Woman," he retorted, "of course I didn't know. I have had no experience in such matters. Your mother had to tell me."

She gave him a wan smile.

"Well, now you know," she said.

"Yes, now I know," he agreed, "and we must see to it that you have plenty of rest. You must not lift heavy burdens or help with the housework. You must have proper food."

Her smile turned into laughter. "Mother will take all proper precautions. She has had vast experience," she assured him.

Although he had not been too happy to have Mrs. Bowes a permanent resident in his home he was glad now that she was living with them. She knew what to do. He could depend upon her. He walked on clouds. Wonder of wonders, he was to be a father! Smugly he confided to Calvin the news.

Calvin vouchsafed a thin-lipped smile.

"It happens all of the time," he said.

"But not to me," Knox retorted.

"We are glad that the babe will be born in Geneva," Calvin remarked. "Truly, the child will be well favored."

"Aye," John acknowledged proudly.

John had to set the news down in letter form to all of his correspondents. And that eventually caused a flood of letters to him. From Scotland and England came epistles requesting advice on the approved methods of rearing children.

He had brought with him from Scotland a young man by the name of Patrick and between them they devised something of a form letter to send to many of the women who wrote him.

Patrick laughed one day as he sat down to this chore. "Some of these epistles are so intimate that I shall have to get married myself if I am to answer them adequately."

"I think that I did better in my replies before I was married," John told him. "I knew everything about marriage and the nurture of children before I became a husband and father — nay, I know that I am not yet a father, but even the prospect of being one affrights me — and now I am not certain that I have the answers to their questions. You can do better without experience than I can with."

Christopher Goodman offered to take Knox's preaching assignments but John told him that he thought he could handle them without difficulty until Marjory's time arrived.

But the fact that he was to become a father undoubtedly influenced his preaching. He began to see that the Christian home would be a vital factor in building a permanent Reformation. It was not enough to convert a nation. The homes of the nation needed to share in this vital experience. They needed to be an integral part of it.

The beautiful Christmas story assumed a tremendous importance for him. Because of Rome's exaltation of the status of Mary, the mother of Jesus, Knox had unconsciously begun to discount her genuine place in the story of the birth of Christ. She had almost come to represent to him much of what he regarded as wrong in the church.

Now he began to recognize her with wonder and awe as the consecrated vessel by which God had planned to bring His Son into the world. The fact that she was a simple countrywoman and yet had been chosen to be the means by which the Son of God came into the world made him consider her with a new sense of the dignity of womanhood.

Contrasting Mary, the mother of Jesus, with the two Marys who were then ruling England and Scotland, one as the queen, the other as the queen regent, may have been partly responsible for two letters which he began to compose.

One was an elaboration of the *pasquil* which the queen regent of Scotland had treated with such scorn. The other was in reality a pamphlet which he entitled, *The First Blast of the Trumpet against the Monstrous Regiment of Women.* In Knox's usage "regiment" meant "regimen," or "reign," or "rule."

The elaboration of the *pasquil* occupied him for some time. Apparently that which most troubled John was the scorn and levity with which the queen regent had treated the first letter. When he had learned of her attitude it had cut him to the quick. If she had objected to it violently, if she had publicly condemned him for writing it, her action would have disturbed him much less than the contempt with which she had received the missive.

Thus he began his second letter by saying, "The avarice and cruelty which you yourself have shown, together with the cruelty of those others whom you have placed in authority over Scotland, are known by the facts. The conspiracies and conjurings of your false prophets are known to the world. But in all your realm no one is found so faithful to God, nor merciful to your grace, as will dare admonish you to repent before God Himself shall rise in judgment over you."

Thereafter he repeated the charges that he had made in the first letter but closed the epistle by reaffirming his loyalty to the throne of Scotland. It was significant, however, that his pledge of allegiance was not to the person of the queen regent but to the institution of the crown. This letter he dispatched to Scotland with instructions that it should be delivered to James Balfour who would know how to arrange for it to be laid before the queen regent.

The First Blast of the Trumpet against the Monstrous Regiment of Women required a long time in preparation. Undoubtedly the scorn with which Mary of Lorraine had received his letter was one of the factors which occasioned its writing. The fact that he had to flee England and that many of his friends had been ordered beheaded or burned by Mary Tudor in England was another factor. The knowledge that a young woman was being groomed in France to occupy the throne of Scotland was a third.

It is also possible that the dominance of his mother-in-law, Elizabeth Bowes, was an added cause. He regarded her with great affection but he frequently became tired of her complaints. And, although he had appreciated Mrs. Bowes' willingness to espouse his cause with her daughter, he probably felt that if Richard Bowes had not been so put upon by his wife he would not have objected as strenuously as he did to his daughter's marriage to John.

He began to feel a sympathy for Richard and to realize that the latter had probably built up a resentment against himself because Mrs. Bowes had so favorably regarded him. In any event he felt that it was unnatural for a woman to rule the household as Mrs. Bowes had so evidently reigned in her home.

John's use of the word "monstrous" is different from modern usage. He meant by it "unnatural." In John's opinion man was born to rule — not woman. A man should be the head of his own household. A man should be the head of state. He believed that a woman's place was in the home and that even there she should but carry out the will of her husband.

This was the position of the Apostle Paul and Knox leaned heavily upon him for authority. John had also been surfeited by the possessiveness of the many women whom he had met in his preaching appointments in both England and Scotland. Because of his eloquence and despite his appearance — or perhaps because of it — many had sought to mother him and they had tired him with their trivial problems.

In any event he was convinced that when a woman was set

in a place of the highest authority in a nation she could become a positive evil. In both England and Scotland good men were being done to death with women on the thrones. If he had been inclined to temper the message which he wrote those facts would have so incensed him that he could not but indicate his disapproval of the women responsible for them and what he regarded as "petticoat rule" in general.

Although he confided frequently in John Calvin and went to him for advice he purposely refrained from discussing the matter of the pamphlet with the latter. Possibly he recalled Calvin's caution when, on an earlier occasion, he had submitted to him a list of four questions which dealt basically with the accession of Mary to the throne. Calvin had referred him to Henry Bullinger and had given him no answer.

There was nothing cautious about the way in which he plunged into the subject. John evidently intended to publish three "Blasts" and not to indicate authorship until he published the third. That one would be published over his signature.

He prefaced the pamphlet by indicating that he would have to count on the indignation not only of those who were interested in the reprobated practice of having a woman govern a nation but also of those gentle spirits among the learned who would be alarmed at the boldness of his attack. He had no doubt that he would be described as "curious, despiteful, a sower of sedition." Conceivably one day he might "perchance be attainted for treason."

"Yet," he wrote, "I intend to cover my eyes and shut my ears against the entreaties of these because there is need that the truth regarding this monstrous practice should be made known to the world."

The burden of his complaint was contained in the words of the first sentence of the *Blast*: "To promote a woman to bear rule, superiority, dominion, or empire, above any realm, nation, or city, is repugnant to nature, contumely to God, a thing most contrarious to His revealed will and approved ordinance, and, finally, of all equity and justice."

He marshaled his arguments from many different sources: the Bible, and particularly the teachings of Paul; the constitutions of the free states of antiquity; the authority of their most celebrated legislators and philosophers; and the practices of the nations of his own time. Before his death Edward VI had himself proposed to the privy council the enactment of a law forbidding the accession of a female to the crown of England. While the law was not enacted many felt that it should have been. In France women were prohibited by law from succeeding to the throne.

The strongest points which he made in developing his theme were: first, that nature intended the female sex to be subject, not superior to the male. This is evident, he noted, from their infirmities, both corporeal and mental. He did note the exception that God, "by singular privilege, and for certain causes, exempted some notable individuals from the common rank of women."

His second point was that the divine law which was announced at the creation of the first pair had expressly assigned to man the dominion over woman. God had, furthermore, commanded the woman to be subject to the man. He added that female government was not permitted among the Jews, that it is contrary to apostolic teaching. Finally, he noted, government by females leads to the perversion of government, and other pernicious consequences.

Whenever his wife or mother-in-law interrupted him in the composition of this treatise he hastily turned to some other work. Apparently John was not altogether convinced that writing this diatribe was altogether wise. Certainly, if he had had no doubts about the matter, he would have shared his thoughts with Calvin but he never mentioned the pamphlet to him and, after its appearance, Calvin was altogether surprised and completely unaware of its authorship.

When finally John had completed the treatise he made arrangements for it to be printed in Frankfurt and from there it was distributed to friends in Scotland and England. It caused a great furore — more so in Scotland than in England, for at the time Mary Tudor was ill and no one dared present to her a copy of the treatise for fear of causing her death.

Soon after its publication she died and Elizabeth succeeded to the throne. While John did not have her in mind when he wrote the pamphlet she assumed that the author had aimed the diatribe at her. Eventually she was to discover the name of the author, and when she did she forbade Knox ever again to set foot on English soil. Once distributed John promptly turned his attention to other duties.

His ministry in Geneva was quiet and uneventful. The church grew as persecution in Scotland and England increased, occasioned in part by the publication of the pamphlet. His friend William Locke of London died, and Mrs. Locke and her family came to Geneva for a protracted visit. While it increased the size of his household it did not put a burden on his purse since Mrs. Locke was well-to-do and contributed much more than her share to housekeeping expenses.

Mrs. Locke also made it a point to take especial care of Marjory as the time for the birth of the baby drew near. John felt somewhat relieved but he was, nevertheless, not too happy about the arrangement for he had little opportunity to see Marjory when they could be alone. The one redeeming circumstance for him was the presence of Patrick and his services as a secretary, but Mrs. Locke's constant care of Marjory made his wife less dependent upon him and in a measure erected a barrier between them.

His home was thrown into a turmoil in April when Mrs. Locke's daughter died and left her inconsolable. John endeavored to minister to her but the more he attempted to comfort her the more demanding she became.

It was, therefore, something of a release when, in May, John's own baby was born. Mrs. Locke continued to bewail the loss of her daughter but, when no one stopped to minister to her, she gave herself to increased activity on behalf of Marjory.

When Marjory's pains started in the middle of the night John was helpless. He aroused the household, sent Patrick for the midwife, and turned over the entire complicated procedure to his mother-in-law, the midwife and Mrs. Locke.

Patrick and John paced the floor.

"You need not remain awake, my son," John told Patrick. "'Tis enough that I am inconvenienced and lose my sleep."

"But I may find something to do for you or the mistress," Patrick suggested hopefully.

"But what would it be?"

"I know not, but something may occur."

"I can't imagine what 'twould be," said John.

"I shall be on hand," Patrick assured him.

"'Tis a strange and fearsome undertaking, this matter of birth," John remarked. "In my boyhood the cattle and sheep brought forth their young without fanfare, but when a human female hath a babe entire households are disrupted and the father, who is responsible for it, cannot even see his wife."

"It's like rabbits," Patrick remarked.

"What is like rabbits, lad?" John asked, his curiosity piqued.

"Why, the birth of a child," Patrick replied. "The mother rabbit pushes the father out of the burrow for fear he will eat the offspring."

"Eh?" ejaculated John. "You mean that the father rabbit would actually . . .?"

"Aye," Patrick replied. "A most horrible thing!"

"It is indeed," John agreed. "But I can assure you, lad, that I have no intention of dining upon my offspring."

It was at this moment that Mrs. Locke made her appearance, holding in her arms a wizened piece of humanity, red and wrinkled.

"A wonderful boy!" she remarked, offering to let John hold the little creature.

"A boy!" he exclaimed, shrinking back from contact with the stranger.

"A boy," she affirmed.

Tentatively, fearfully, he held out his arms and then let them fall.

"I had best not," he explained. "I might drop him."

"Ninny!" she retorted. "He is but a wee baby. He will not bite you. He hath no teeth."

"I know. I know," John replied. "But I have never had experience . . . He might slip. I might . . . No. I had better not."

But she thrust the child into his arms.

Gingerly he accepted the tiny bundle.

"He's so wee!" he remarked.

"Of course. He came into the world just a few moments ago."

"Oh, aye!" John agreed.

"And what will you call the bairn?" she inquired.

"Oh, yes, we must give him a name. He hath none as yet, then?"

"No. You must name him."

John pondered a moment, confidence returning the while.

"Let us call him Nathanael," John announced decisively, "the friend of God. And may God always be his friend, too."

"Amen," Patrick murmured.

A few days after the birth of the child John was visited by two friends from Edinburgh. One of them, Ian Duncan, was the Dean of Guild. The other was Thomas Kinross, a burgess.

They bore a letter signed by Glencairn and three other nobles, Erskine, Lorne and James Stuart.

The missive stated that, while the political situation remained unchanged, the Roman Church was more than ever in disfavor and the queen regent was apparently opposing it herself. They urged him to return to Scotland where he could now stoke the fires of Reformation with greater possibility of their remaining alight than there had been in the past.

In addition to what was set down in the letter, the emissaries brought a message which they did not want to commit to writing. This was a proposal for a renewed effort to obtain freedom of worship for Protestants, and fresh petitions to the regent and Parliament for the reform of the church.

It was a most unpropitious time for John to consider a return to Scotland. Marjory would be in no condition to travel for some time. Mrs. Locke, with the loss of both husband and daughter fresh in her mind, constituted a responsibility which he could not very well escape, and he was most happy in Geneva.

Nevertheless, he promised them that he would consider their proposals and take counsel with the consistory of the church, with Calvin and others, and let them know his answer.

But the first one with whom he conferred was Marjory. He was confident that she would oppose the move and possibly, for that reason, he spoke to her first. She would confirm his own opinion that he should not go.

"Edinburgh!" Marjory exclaimed when he divulged the contents of the letter to her. "Wonderful! Nathanael will grow up among his own countrymen. He'll not be speaking French but the good Scotch tongue."

When Knox broached the subject to Calvin he also agreed.

"I am indeed glad that we have had you this long in Geneva. You have done a good work here," Calvin assured him. "But for the welfare of the church which we hope to see established in your homeland this is the call of God to you."

In this judgment the consistory in Knox's church also agreed. It took John some little time to come to a final decision and his friends waited for him to make up his mind. But Marjory's confinement had not affected her health in any way and there was no good reason why they could not leave. Therefore, he assured the two that as soon as he could leave he would be on his way back to Scotland.

The decision made, he began preparing for the journey. Other factors intervened which occasioned frequent postponements. Knox discovered that France was making plans for an invasion of England. Forces were gathering in the channel ports and it would be difficult to obtain passage. Furthermore, France was daily becoming more pronouncedly Catholic and the king had requested the pope to establish in his country an inquisition similar to the one which had been set up in Spain. The Cardinal of Lorraine, brother of Scotland's queen regent, would become the grand inquisitor.

While nothing ever came of this proposal the king himself issued an edict against heretics in July. Knox would be subject to arrest if he entered or passed through any part of the country.

15

In the light of the dangers which confronted John when he crossed the country with his family he was deeply incensed when he arrived in Dieppe to receive letters from Scotland informing him that there had been considerable change in the situation there since their representatives met with him in May. It was now October and in the interim much had happened.

First of all, the bishops were making attempts to reform the Roman Church from within. While their efforts had not been successful the fact that they recognized the need for reform was significant. The coming of John Knox might dissuade them from the effort which they had made.

There was also considerable talk of war with England and people were losing their concern for the problems of religion and thinking about their national interests. In the event that war did occur it would possibly assume the nature of a religious war. That is, England was now nominally Protestant, with the death of Mary and the accession of Elizabeth, and Scotland was still Roman Catholic. To be aggressively Protestant at that time might seem to be treasonable to Scotland — and Knox could not be Protestant at all without being aggressive.

It is important to note that the invitation which had been sent to John had not been withdrawn. It still stood. The letters which he received were from individuals, some of them signers of the original invitation, to be sure, but writing now in no official capacity, simply as his friends.

They were certainly not responsible for what was happening in Scotland. They had sent the invitation to Knox to come to Scotland in good faith. If changes had occurred in the situation they were not of their making. And they did not indicate that the invitation was being withdrawn. They were writing as his friends — not to discourage him from coming but to apprise him of the conditions which he would face. If John had not been married, if he had not so recently become a father, they would probably not have written as they did, but these friends felt that they would be responsible for his family's welfare if he should respond to the invitation which they had extended months before.

In any event their letters incensed John. He had traveled across France to Dieppe at considerable danger. He had cut the ties which had bound him to the church and to friends in Geneva, and now the people who had invited him to come were telling him that the time was not just ripe.

The more John read the more aroused he became. When he sat down to write to the friends in Edinburgh, therefore, the epistle which he indited was bitingly sarcastic. He reminded them that he had given up his church in Geneva; he had traveled across a hostile France; his life and the lives of his wife and child were in constant danger. Were they so indifferent to the welfare of himself and his family that they would permit them to make such sacrifices and then, at the last moment, inform him that the time for his coming was not propitious?

His letter was replete with hints concerning plagues and punishments which God would visit upon the wicked on this earth — without even considering those far greater torments which sinners would suffer in hell. Since those who had invited him were members of the nobility his rebuke was for all members of this class. He concluded the epistle by asserting that, while they might regard his words as sharp and indiscreetly spoken, he was writing as a true friend. One who was such a friend and not a flatterer could do nothing else.

It is interesting to note, however, that, far from arousing their indignation, his friends felt that John's rebuke was justified. Consequently they met and signed a "Common Band," making solemn pledges in it that they would strive for the cause of reformation even unto death. When Knox heard of this move

and realized the circumstances which had occasioned their letters
he expressed his sorrow to them for having written as he did.

There was a further element in the situation, to be sure. There
had been so many farewells in Geneva, so many expressions of
appreciation for his services, that to return there would be in
the nature of an anticlimax. A return to Geneva would injure
his pride, and might even make him appear ridiculous. John
could stand opposition. He could take physical blows. But it
was difficult to accept a situation in which he would be subject
to ridicule.

He did not, therefore, return at once to the Swiss city. For
one thing, the embarrassment which it would occasion evidently
deterred him. But certain of the French churches were also
eager to hear him and he spent some time preaching to the
French Protestant congregations in Rochelle and Dieppe, and
occasionally also to the English congregation in the latter seaport.

The other reason for his failure to return immediately to
Geneva was the difficulties which he would face when traveling
across France. The French monarch's edict regarding heretics
was not being carried out in such places as Dieppe and Rochelle
but if John were to take his family across country it was quite
possible that he would be apprehended by agents of the crown.
The fact, also, that the baby was still so young made him hesitate to leave the comparative security of lodgings in Dieppe
to risk wintertime travel across France.

It was, therefore, not until March that John set out with Marjory, Mrs. Bowes, and his baby son, for Geneva. When he arrived there he began another period of letter writing, probably
the most prolific in his career.

He had an unexpected response to his letter to the nobility
which had been written in haste and chagrin but had had a
most sympathetic and earnest hearing from its recipients. They
informed him of their compact and of the manner in which
it had stiffened the resolution of the nobles to accomplish a
real reformation in Scotland. They renewed their invitation to
John to return to Scotland, promising their most earnest support.

In order to secure Calvin's influence they also wrote him,
telling him about the misunderstandings which had arisen because of the letters which certain among them had written and
urging him to use his influence to persuade Knox to return to
Edinburgh. Because of the political situation in the country,
however, the letters did not reach Geneva until the following

November, almost a year after the meeting was held and the letters written.

During this period John was busy once more with the work of the church and with his study and prolific writing. He also found time to enjoy his baby. Like any proud father he dandled the child on his knee and even tried to sing to him. Never one to carry a tune, this was not too successful.

Nathanael's lower lip would quiver and tears come into his eyes when John's voice boomed out in a hymn or some other song.

"You frighten the bairn, husband," Marjory would say, taking the babe into her own arms.

"Foolishness!" John would exclaim. "My voice is soothing to his ears. He weeps because there is so much other noise about him. The gabble of women frightens the bairn."

Early in 1558 Marjory also informed him that he would be a father once more.

"Another child in Geneva?" John exclaimed in dismay. "I had hoped that our next might be born in Scotland."

"He will be a Scot ne'ertheless," Marjory assured him.

"But Nathanael's first words sound more French than Scotch," John protested.

"Like all babes he has a language all his own," Marjory replied sagely.

It was early in 1558 that John set to work on additional pamphlets. Having launched his *Blast* months before, he made it the foundation for his *Appellation* which was addressed to the nobles, and his *Letter to the Commonalty of Scotland*. The "commonalty" to whom John wrote consisted basically of the growing middle class, the tradesmen in the cities and towns, the free-holding farmers of the countryside.

Scotland had a larger middle class in proportion to its population than England or France or any other European country. The average Scotsman was more independent than the citizens of other lands. The nobles were far more democratic in their outlook and mingled much more freely with the middle class. Consequently the "commonalty" had much greater power. John realized that it would be advisable to win this group if the Reformation were to succeed.

The *Appellation* was a spirited defense of himself against the condemnation of the Scotch bishops. It was literally an appeal from the judgment which the latter had visited upon him. John had it printed and distributed to the lairds in all of Scotland.

Knox was essentially conservative in his politics. He believed in the doctrine of the divine right of the sovereign to rule. People only had the right to rebel against the sovereign if the monarch had flagrantly transgressed against justice. And, in the event of such transgression, it was not only the right but the duty of people to rebel. In every man there is an inherent knowledge of what is right and just. When this is violated it should be the responsibility of the nobility to bring the monarch to task. This was all within what Knox regarded as the realm of natural law. But Knox was concerned also with what he called the "moral" law. This was "the constant and unchangeable will of God" as revealed in the Scriptures.

This is the basic law of God and no man-made law may supersede it or improve upon it. Not only must the individual obey this "moral" law, but he is obligated to defend it against contravention by others, whether they are people in ordinary circumstances or rulers. And no truly spiritually-minded individual should permit either prince or pauper to frame laws which are inconsistent with it.

Knox then came to the subject of this moral law. According to the Scriptures, he believed, no woman, in the ordinary course of human events, should be permitted to rule over a nation. Occasionally there might be an exception, as was Deborah, who lived in the time of the Judges and was herself so designated. Her case was one of special divine ordinance. God, the source of the laws which He Himself makes, may occasionally promulgate special legislation governing specific cases, or He may suspend the operation of law and bring a miracle to pass.

No one, however, should act as if such special legislation on the part of The Eternal against the ordinary course of the divine providence was common. Since the reign of the queen regent was clearly not a miracle like the judgeship of Deborah in the Old Testament it was not only a proper course for the nobles to take but it was their positive duty to remove the queen regent and to execute the death sentence on any who would defend her.

Even though a subject should have taken an oath of fealty to support her he should not be excused from executing that which was manifestly his duty. Such an oath should be broken in light of the fact that it is contrary to God's law. Furthermore, since a queen has no lawful authority to reign, an oath of that nature is null and void. Nor could a queen confer to anyone else, authority which, according to God's law, she does not possess. This, he believed, would take care of the young Mary's marriage to the French dauphin.

This document reveals the lengths to which John was ready to go in fulfilling the mission to which he felt he had been called by God. The position which he took was, by ordinary standards, treason, and if the letter would fall into the hands of his enemies it would be manifest evidence of his guilt. By this time John was ready to go to any lengths to bring about the establishment of the Reformation in Scotland.

His letter to the commonalty further developed his thesis. In both Scotland and England the middle classes had nothing to do with government. But Knox laid down the thesis that the responsibility for dealing with corruption and idolatry rested as heavily on the shoulders of the middle classes as upon the nobles. The group which they represented were in duty bound to unite with the nobles in compelling the bishops to cease their tyranny over the souls of men.

Furthermore, they had a particularly pressing duty to demand true pastors for the churches in which they worshiped. Perhaps, without recognizing it, John was laying down at the time one of the foundation stones on which the Protestant Church was to build. For one of the basic tenets of Protestantism in all of its branches is the right of the people to choose their own pastors. This is sometimes delegated but is inherent in Protestantism.

He laid down some practical suggestions for the manner in which the commonalty might register their protests against pastors whom they did not approve. One such was to refuse to pay tithes. "Ye may, moreover," he wrote, "withhold the fruits and profits which your false bishops and clergy most unjustly receive of you, until such time as they be compelled faithfully to do their charge and duties, which is to preach unto you Christ Jesus truly, rightly to minister His sacraments according to His own institution, and so to watch for the salvation of your souls, as is commanded by Christ Jesus Himself and by His apostles, Peter and Paul."

Knox was actually setting forth in both of these documents an argument justifying revolution. The people of Scotland were in subjection to tyranny on the part of both church and crown and, because of this fact, extreme measures for the overthrow of tyranny were justified. He probably realized that in the train of revolution would come looting, wanton murder and other extremes; but he did not realize the extent to which these would eventually go.

In November, 1558, Mary Tudor, who had earned the unhappy but well-deserved sobriquet of "Bloody Mary," died, and Elizabeth succeeded to the throne. Her death meant that Protestants on the continent could return to their homes in England since Elizabeth was known to be altogether Protestant in her sympathies. The members of John's congregation in Geneva were among the number who wished to return to their home island. There was so much excitement that the services began to decrease in size as people picked up their belongings and started for home.

John resolved that he would return to Scotland but would visit England en route. Remembering his previous disappointment at Dieppe, he decided that he would leave his family in Geneva and go alone to Dieppe to book passage, taking with him only Patrick. There was less danger than there had been earlier but he was responsible for the Locke family as well as his own.

When John arrived in Dieppe he found turmoil similar to that which had prevailed in Geneva. The English colony was excited over the news and was making plans to return to the home country. From all parts of Germany and from France the jubilant refugees came to seek return passage to England.

John sought to obtain from Queen Elizabeth a passport which would permit him to pass through England. He wanted to take the Locke family to London, and he also desired to visit friends and members of his wife's family in Berwick. He was by now accustomed to the idea that Mrs. Bowes would be a permanent addition to his family but he felt that she should at least have an opportunity to see her children before they set out for Scotland.

Furthermore, he probably felt a reluctance to venture into Scotland until he could first ascertain how he would be received. England, under Elizabeth, was now thoroughly Protestant but Scotland, under the regent, was still Catholic and he had no desire to spend another period as a galley slave.

John arrived in Dieppe in January, 1559, and immediately set about the task of securing the passport. Possibly because Elizabeth assumed that his diatribe against *The Monstrous Regiment of Women* had been written with her in mind she refused to grant him passage. He waited for several months in vain, seeking through the influence of a friend, Lord Cecil, to gain the coveted document, but Queen Elizabeth ignored him completely. Meanwhile Marjory was having her second baby whom John eventually named Eleazar. She was well enough to travel in April and by easy stages she came to Dieppe with Mrs. Locke and Mrs. Bowes. Despairing of receiving his passport, John made arrangements to go directly to Scotland. They secured passage and he arrived in Edinburgh with his entourage the second of May.

He had left Scotland thirteen years before at the age of thirty-three. Now he was forty-six. He had visited his homeland only occasionally during those years but upon his return he was acclaimed as the leader of the Reformation cause.

However, it was a sorry crew which he was called upon to lead. Many of the nobles who were nominally Protestant could be bought. Others were unstable. He had scarcely landed in Scotland when, by edict of the queen regent, he was proclaimed an outlaw.

But, learning that there was to be a great mass meeting of Protestants in Stirling just a week after his arrival, he left his family in Edinburgh after first seeing Mrs. Locke and her family off for London.

Learning that the queen regent intended to prevent the holding of the meeting, Knox decided not to attempt to go to Stirling but went instead to Perth. But even at Perth the nobles were conspicuous by their absence, intimidated by the crown. Yet the meeting in Perth did attract a considerable number of people, a motley crew which had been stirred into action by the nobles. John preached a rousing sermon in the Church of St. John the Baptist and the people were so stirred by it that they proceeded to loot the three monasteries in the town.

This was the signal for warfare.

The queen regent rallied her followers, including the French army which she had at her command. Knox's friends among the nobles, hearing that a French army was marching on Perth, had a change of heart and came to Perth to resist what they regarded as foreign aggression.

Knox sent a communication to the queen regent, reaffirming his loyalty but demanding liberty of worship. To the nobles who were still absent Knox wrote, insisting that now was the time to come to the cause openly. The message was so urgent that throngs responded, ready for a pitched battle, if need be, with the soldiers of the crown.

But the regent had no desire for civil war. She, therefore, sent two emissaries who, for a considerable time, had been counted as among the most stalwart in the reformation party, Lord James Stuart and the Duke of Argyll. They were instructed by the regent to promise Knox that if the Protestant army would march out of Perth she would not allow a single French soldier to occupy the city. Argyll and Stuart added their own promises that if the regent would break her word they would come over to the Protestant forces.

Knox accepted the terms, albeit with misgiving. Mary entered the city at the head of her troops. The occupying forces were not French but, instead, Scots in the pay of France. During the occupation a child was killed by one of her soldiers, and she dismissed the town council. Argyll and Stuart were convinced that the regent's promises were not to be trusted and came over to the side of Knox.

At about this time John bethought himself of the statement that he had made to Sir James Balfour that he would some day preach again in the parish kirk at St. Andrews and resolved that the time had come for him to do so. While his army had been bivouacked in Perth and after they had left the city to encamp in the countryside, Knox was preaching. Once more his sermons had all the fire of his earlier ministry. In Craill and Anstruther he won men to his cause, not only to give their tacit consent to the Reformation but to take up arms in the cause. He was another Peter the Hermit, challenging, wooing men to engage in a holy war. Now he determined that his next preaching would be in St. Andrews.

Archbishop Hamilton had his residence there, and the ecclesiastic determined to oppose Knox with force. John heard that the archbishop would be ready with troops to meet his challenge but he insisted that he wanted no protection. He needed no army at his back. He would leave the matter of protection to The Eternal.

Thus he returned to St. Andrews to preach one of his most rousing sermons. He took for his text the incident of the moneychangers in the temple. Christ had expelled them from the house of the Lord. Were not his hearers also charged to follow Jesus' example and expel those who, fifteen centuries later, were defiling God's house? The archbishop had threatened to send him to the stake if he should preach but, afraid of the multitude, failed to fulfill his threats. Instead, he scurried off to Edinburgh to inform the queen regent that John had taken over the pulpit in his cathedral church.

Mary again assembled her troops. Argyll and Lord James Stuart, her erstwhile emissaries, gathered their men at Cupar, about ten miles from St. Andrews, resolved to protect Knox. Meanwhile Knox continued with his preaching. The Protestant troops at Cupar numbered less than two hundred. But suddenly, one night, from Angus, north of the Tay, and from the Lothians, Protestant levies appeared, ready to do battle against the queen regent's troops.

These troops retreated, pursued by the Protestants. Looting of churches and monasteries by the latter — or at least by their camp followers — was carried on in every town through which they passed. For the Protestants had no regular discipline as an army. They were rude, rough men from the highlands, peasants from the lowlands, now expressing their feelings for the church and for the French regent whom they despised.

Mary appealed to Henry II, King of France, but he was busy at home and unwilling to engage his troops in Scotland for what, he suspected, might be a losing cause. She then pleaded for the presence of her daughter Mary, later to be known as "Queen of Scots," but her plea came to Henry II at about the time that he was killed in a tournament. Mary's husband, a sickly, adolescent moron, succeeded to the throne.

Before anyone in authority in France could reply to Mary's plea, Edinburgh was seized and on Saturday, the first of July, 1559, John Knox preached in the cathedral of St. Giles, the leading church of Scotland.

When word of the pillage of churches and monasteries reached Calvin he was horror-stricken. It cannot be said that Knox had encouraged such actions on the part of the men who had rallied to his banner, but it is quite evident that his preaching had inflamed men's passions and they were able to excuse their excesses by pointing out that Knox had so roundly condemned the priests and prelates that they were only visiting upon evil men the punishment which they richly deserved.

Nor can it be said that Knox actively discouraged such pillage. Whether he could have held in check the rude multitude which had rallied to the Reformation banner even if he had desired to do so is problematic. In any event there is little evidence to indicate that he actively sought to dissuade them.

But it must be pointed out that it had become a bitter war with excesses committed on both sides, and certainly the memories of the martyrs who had burned at the stake were ever fresh in the minds of the rude and rough Scots and they were resolved to avenge the atrocities which had been committed.

16

Upon his arrival in Scotland John had taken up residence in the cottage in the courtyard of Douglas Mackenzie's home which, although it had the appearance of an ordinary abode, was more like a medieval castle. Marjory, Mrs. Bowes and the two Knox sons lived there in comparative security while the events in the north were transpiring.

Mrs. Bowes at last tired of her life in such restricted circumstances and when John returned to Edinburgh she decided to go back to Berwick to take up the reins of motherhood. John had become so accustomed to her spells of melancholia and her frequent complaints that when she left he was actually sorry to see her go. Added to this, Marjory was not well and the presence of Mrs. Bowes in the home meant that the household ran smoothly.

Marjory, too, had leaned upon her mother for counsel and advice all through the years. Earlier she had not been happy with the restrictions which her mother had imposed upon her but when she was gone Marjory greatly missed her.

John was so preoccupied with the political situation and with the preparation of the fiery sermons which he preached Sunday after Sunday in St. Giles that he had little time for his family.

"I had thought, when you began preaching here, that we might have more time for one another and for the bairns," Marjory wistfully remarked on one occasion as they were dining.

John had brought a manuscript to the table and, even as he consumed the food which had been set before him and which he scarcely tasted, was busy revising it.

"Yes, dear," he agreed.

"You have not even heard what I have said," she remarked.

"Yes, dear," he replied automatically.

Marjory raised her voice, "You say, 'Yes, dear,' but you pay no attention."

John raised his head. "What were you saying?" he inquired.

"I knew it," Marjory retorted. "You agree with everything because you have no idea what I say."

John looked puzzled.

"I remarked that I wished that we might live as a family," Marjory explained. "You are gone from home so much of the time that when you are here you are involved in conferences with friends and you pay no attention to us."

John was about to turn back to perusal of his manuscript but somehow her objection managed to reach him.

"Eh!" he exclaimed. "Are we not together as a family now? Are we not altogether happy, dearest one? To be sure, I'm a dour Scot and not much inclined to reveal what is on my heart. But thou knowest how deeply I love you."

Marjory sighed.

"To be sure," she agreed. "Mayhap I miss my mother for she was always at hand for conversation."

"Aye," John agreed ruefully. "That she was. Sometimes it was almost overwhelming."

"It was that in truth. But now there is no one but the children with whom I can converse. Even when we are at the table you are immersed in sermons, or letters, or plans for the Reformation."

"Oh, aye, my sweet, but the time will come when we shall have won out and then I can be more of a husband."

"And a father," she reminded him. "You have scarce a moment for our sons."

"Aye. I should spend some time with them."

But he had little opportunity for this. Men came and went from his study. There were plots and counterplots. Perhaps, even if he had had time to give to his family, he would not have known what to do with it, for fatherhood had come to him late in life. John could not avoid the obligations which his leadership imposed upon him.

St. Giles became more and more the sounding board for the Reformation. The queen regent sought to deny him this pulpit but he paid her scant heed. Alternately the Protestants and the regent's troops commanded the city. Knox still had St. Giles.

Finally, on October 24, 1559, the Lords of the Congregation deposed Mary as queen regent. The charges against her were that she had conspired to make Scotland a vassal of France. The order of deposition was read from the Mercat Cross. Since Scotland was definitely a royalist country the Lords informed the people of the country that the young Mary had indicated that she was ready to begin her reign. Further to strengthen their hand the Lords prepared a long document in Latin recounting the wrongs which had been done to Scotland by Mary of Guise, and their intention to bring the young queen from France at the earliest possible moment to assume the throne.

It was purely an expedient which the lords thought necessary to keep from being invaded by the armies of other nations. The absentee queen, since she was absent, was a far better monarch than the regent who was in Scotland.

However, deposing the queen regent was not disposing of her. For the next year it was nip and tuck as to whether the queen regent would win the aid of Frenchmen or if the Reformation group would be victorious with the help of English funds. Elizabeth did not want to send troops to the aid of Scotland for fear of entering upon a war with France but she was willing to encourage the Scots in their warfare short of British involvement. She also hesitated to begin what might become a religious war.

John also sought to withdraw from the political arena. He had never desired to enter it and he discovered that it meant alliances with men who proclaimed themselves adherents of the Reformation but were involved in the Reformation only for personal gain.

Marjory's pleas also could not be disregarded. He was eager to accede to her wishes and give more time to her and the family. When he was running hither and yon for conferences with politicians and statesmen he could neither be a husband and father nor could he be a preacher with a message.

And as he grew older he would have preferred preaching sermons on the great themes of Christian faith: justification, salvation, the love and mercy of God. Knox was by nature a gentle man. He was even inclined to give Mary of Lorraine another opportunity to reign on condition that she would repent of her past conduct. But he was overruled by the Lords of the Congregation.

Actually the lairds were glad to use him for their own purposes but they paid scant heed to his messages. There were exceptions among them: Sir James Balfour and Erskine of Dun being notable, but others who had been attracted to the cause of the Reformation were altogether self-seeking and eager for personal gain.

Although he sought to keep out of the political situation the nobles realized that Knox was their principal asset and he was kept busy negotiating with the British. He finally secured help from Britain, and a treaty of mutual defense was signed by representatives of Scotland and England. The Scots guaranteed good faith by giving hostages to England. It was the beginning of the end for the queen regent and on June 10, 1560, she died of dropsy.

John burst into his home when he heard the news.

"The last enemy of the true faith has finally gone," he announced to Marjory. "Mary of Guise is dead and Scotland is free."

Marjory received the news with scant enthusiasm.

"Do ye not ken what it means?" he inquired, appalled by her lack of interest.

"I hope that I do," Marjory replied listlessly. "I hope it means an end to your traveling. I hope that it means you can now be a father and a preacher."

John glanced at her anxiously.

"Have I failed you so much?" he asked contritely.

"No," she replied, "you have never failed me, dear heart. It is just that I feel so listless, as if life were ebbing away from me. Now we can be together again and I may be better."

Knox devoutly hoped that such might be the case. Despite his own poor health, however, he continued his activity. He began a series of sermons early in August with texts from the book of Haggai, the theme of the series being the rebuilding of the temple.

Parliament met at the same time. The majority of its members were Protestant but they were imbued with a sincere desire to allow the free exercise of religion to both the Protestant and Catholic faiths. One great handicap towards the realization of that end was that there were so few Catholic bishops who were regarded by their own people as worthy men. One bishop was a bastard son of the late King James. Several of the bishops had become Protestant. One, Bishop Chisholm, was notoriously the father of numerous bastard sons, all of whom were being amply supported out of the patrimony of the church.

John was invited by parliament to formulate a statement of

Christian doctrine and discipline as the head of a committee appointed for that purpose. It was a task altogether to his liking. In a sense he had been preparing for it for years. But it kept him so preoccupied that he had less time for Marjory than ever before.

Comparatively few objected to the confession as it was drawn up, but among the objectors were Archbishop Hamilton, and Bishops Chisholm and Crichton. Early in August also Parliament passed three acts. The first took Scotland forever out of the jurisdiction of the Pope. The second condemned all forms of doctrine and religious practices which were contrary to the principles of the Reformed faith. The third forbade the celebration of the mass. Penalties for a violation of the latter law were exceedingly severe. For a first offense the punishment was confiscation of goods: for the second, exile: for the third, death.

John did not favor the extremes to which Parliament had gone and was definitely opposed to the efforts of the lords to confiscate all church properties, giving them to the nobility.

He was involved in all of this legislation although he had no vote in Parliament. As a result he had less, rather than more, time to spend with his family. The welfare of Scotland seemed to depend upon his activity and he felt that he must spend the time in furthering both the ecclesiastical and the political aims of the Reformation.

Marjory refrained from urging him any longer to give a portion of his time to his family. That she was ill was altogether evident but John little realized how ill she was. In considerable measure, too, she had lost the will to live. Undoubtedly she was homesick for her mother and for the other members of her family. And Scotland seemed a hard land in which to live.

Early in December she began to run a fever. John thought that she was suffering from one of the colds so prevalent in damp, chilly Edinburgh. He spent as much time as he could at her bedside and engaged several servants to care for the house.

Late one evening he returned from a conference of church leaders to be told by the housekeeper that "Mistress Marjory is sair ill." He went at once to her bedside but she was gasping for air. A few minutes after he arrived she flashed him a warm smile, the first he had seen on her bonny face for months, but soon her breathing began to diminish and within a short time the one love of his life gasped and the end came.

John was plunged into despair by contemplation of his loss.

He reproached himself for having so long neglected her. His friends sought to console him but they could help him little. Even a letter from John Calvin failed to give him comfort. Deep lines were etched in his face. He walked the streets of the city late at night, his figure even more hunched than it had been before.

"Marjory! Marjory!" he would mutter under his breath.

For some time he considered whether or not he should ask Mrs. Bowes to return to Edinburgh to look after his two sons but eventually decided not to do so. He was in no frame of mind to hear her constant complaints, her frequent references to the death of Richard. He resolved to do his best without her aid, keeping on the servants who had been engaged.

At about this same time word came from France that the young king, Mary's husband, had died. That meant that she would probably soon come to Scotland. John felt that this boded well for the Reformation. Mary was only eighteen years of age and he believed that she would be pliable. Freed from the ties to France, she could become a queen who would, with the advice of able Reformation counselors, be able to govern Scotland wisely.

He forgot, for the moment, his aversion to "the monstrous regiment of women." Perhaps he failed to consider that this slip of a girl could even be considered as a person of the female sex. Possibly he unconsciously transferred some of the warm affection that he felt for Marjory to the person of the new sovereign, imagining that she possessed qualities and attitudes which were not hers at all.

He even dreamed of marrying her to one of the Protestant nobles. Surely a mere slip of a girl could be expected to listen to the wise counsel of a man of such wisdom as John Knox. He naturally had in mind the influence that he had exerted upon women of many different ages and stations in life. If they had come to him in the past, Scotch and English women of high and low degree, she could surely be depended upon to listen eagerly to his preaching and seek him out for counsel in the affairs of the realm.

He was unaware of a long conference which the young queen had had with the pope. He didn't even consider that Mary would remember the manner in which he had fought with her mother. After all, the young queen had scarcely known the queen regent since the latter had never left Scotland during the years of her regency and Marie Stuart had not set foot in the country since her early childhood when she had been sent to France for her education.

It was not until the overtures of Arran to the young queen were summarily dismissed that he apparently began to realize that all would not be smooth sailing when she came to Scotland to assume the throne. Then he began to feel that the accession of Marie Stuart would not herald a new day for his country. He preached a sermon in St. Giles warning his hearers against assuming that Scotland's years of trouble and distress would be over. From a feeling of warm security he himself began to feel that the arrival of the youthful monarch might herald instead a period of even greater difficulty than the times through which the country had passed.

In the meantime he began to shore up the gains which had been made. Parliament passed numerous measures which were designed to make the land altogether Protestant. The kirk itself was organized on democratic lines. The people were to choose the ministers of their churches. Education was to be universal. Each child in Scotland was to receive a minimum of four years of schooling, the first such system of universal education in the world. By the time that Mary was to arrive in Scotland Knox and the Reformation leaders felt that they had built a bulwark against the church of which she was a member which could never be breached.

They had considerable time to make these preparations, for it was not until in August of 1561 that Mary reached the shores of her kingdom. On the nineteenth of the month a considerable flotilla of ships from France anchored in the Firth of Forth. They arrived in weather so bad that no one could recall storms and fogs to equal it. Knox announced gloomily that it was a sign from God of the sorrow, dolor, darkness and impiety which her reign heralded.

A salute of cannon announced her arrival at Leith, the sound of which could be heard in Edinburgh. Knox's optimism of six months earlier was completely dissipated.

It is probable that Mary herself felt much as John did. She had heard so much of the monster, Knox, that he typified for her the enemy who would thwart her at every step. It must be said for the young queen that while she feared John Knox she did not hesitate to accept what was, for her, the clear call of duty. She had been destined from birth to rule Scotland, and rule she would. She was altogether imbued with the doctrine of the divine right of kings — and queens — to reign. And whoever challenged that right was an enemy who must be fought and conquered.

Any possibility of a friendly relationship between Mary and Knox had been completely done away before ever her ship cast anchor.

Mary had debarked on Tuesday, the nineteenth. On Sunday, August twenty-fourth, mass was said in the royal chapel at Holyrood. Mary had brought her own chaplain with her from France. Celebration of the mass was definitely contrary to the laws which Parliament had passed. Her chaplain, according to the decree, would lose all his possessions. If he celebrated it a second time he would be subject to exile. The third time the penalty would be death.

But Mary published a royal decree on the twenty-fifth. No one was to molest or trouble in any way any member of the royal household. There could be no alteration or innovation in the matter of the religion of the palace. The devotional life of the queen's household was to be carried on, without hindrance, subject to the desires of the queen.

Martin Luther had agreed to a principle by which the religion of a ruler would become the religion of his subjects. Not so John Knox. Scotland, by the will of the people, had become Protestant. Protestant it would be.

The next Sunday, August thirty-first, Knox preached a rousing sermon in St. Giles. "Better ten thousand armed foes than one mass," he said. "Better that Mary had brought with her a French army than a French chaplain."

Mary was not in attendance upon this service, but her minions were. One such reported the sermon to her majesty.

"He is the most dangerous man in the kingdom," he said. "And the cathedral was filled with people."

"Summon him to the palace," she commanded. "We shall soon see who is the ruler of Scotland."

A short time later, however, she countermanded the order.

"Nay, do not summon him. We shall ignore him instead. To dignify his rantings by personally rebuking him will only encourage him."

The next Sunday the cathedral was filled once more. Again Knox called upon the queen to give up her affiliation with Rome and become one with her subjects.

When she heard a report of the sermon the queen flew into a towering rage.

"Does he presume to dictate to me what I shall believe?" Mary demanded imperiously. "Summon him to the palace."

Marie Stuart was naturally a gentle, kindly person, but she had been brought up in the court of France like a spoiled child; and she could brook no interference with what she felt were her rights and prerogatives as a monarch. Particularly did she feel that her religion was a personal matter with which no one could interfere.

Both Knox and Mary were tense when they faced one another. John felt that he was battling for the cause of the Lord. She believed that she was fighting for her rights and privileges as a monarch. Each felt that his or her stand was one which would promote the welfare of Scotland. John was a perfectionist who would continually strive for that which he regarded as altogether right and just. She was basically an idealist who clung to what she regarded as best for her people and for herself as their monarch. Each faced the battle fearfully. John was afraid that what he might say would widen the breach which was separating Mary from her people. She feared John Knox more than the powers of darkness. The conference between them was thus certain to begin on an uneasy note.

Marie Stuart opened their conversation with an accusation.

"You are the author of that terrible document which you called, *The Monstrous Regiment of Women.* You do not have the temerity to deny its authorship, do you?"

"Nay. I do not deny that I wrote it," John replied quietly, "and I should be willing to recant it if the arguments which I advanced in the pamphlet could be refuted; but I know that no men of repute in the field of letters can prove them false."

"And you do not deny that you drove my mother from her regency?"

"I cannot say that I did such," John replied, "for I do not have the authority or power to make or unmake monarchs. But I freely acknowledge that I was on the side of those who opposed her for she sought to make Scotland a nation of idolaters."

"And you had not read in Holy Writ that God commanded subjects to obey their rulers? Even Martin Luther, heretic though he was, acknowledged the divine requirement that the religion of a nation should be that of the sovereign."

"Ah, but, your majesty, no people are commanded by God to

follow false gods. Were it otherwise God would have commanded the Israelites to worship the gods of the Pharaohs. Instead, he led them out of Egypt back to a land in which they
could worship the Lord God freely. If subjects should always
accept the religion of their monarchs then the early Christians
in Rome should have adopted the false religion of the Caesars."

"Yet they did not lift up sword against the rulers. They refused to take up arms against the Caesars," she said triumphantly.

"True, madam," he replied, "but you cannot deny that they
resisted. Those who refuse to obey royal decrees, whether they
bear arms or not, resist."

Cleverly she pressed home the point. The early Christians did
not bear arms, but the Protestants of Scotland had actually
thrown an army, nondescript though it was, against the queen's
forces.

It is probable that Knox had hoped for some such answer for
it gave him an opportunity to launch into a denunciation of the
Roman Church which he called "the Roman harlot."

"Marvel not," he said, "that I call Rome a harlot; for that
church is altogether polluted with all kinds of spiritual fornica-
tion, as well in doctrine as in manners. Yea, madam, I tell you
that the Church of the Jews which crucified the Lord Jesus
Christ was not so far degenerated from the laws of God, given
through Moses and Aaron, as has the Church of Rome, for in
the last five hundred years she has constantly declined from the
purity of religion which the apostles taught."

"My conscience does not tell me so," she retorted.

"Conscience, madam, requires knowledge," he replied, "and
I fear that right knowledge have ye none."

The argument continued, Queen Mary alternately angered and
dissolved into tears. John's sympathies were aroused by her
plight but he felt the need to adopt drastic measures if he would
make her realize her duty to her realm and win her to the cause
in which he believed with heart and soul. He wanted her to
have the experience which had been his own for he, too, had
once been an adherent of the church to which she was giving
allegiance and he had had to be checked sharply before taking
his stand for the Reformation cause.

Nothing was decided as a result of the conference. Neither
John nor the queen retreated an inch. The issue was joined. The
middle-aged reformer was defying the young queen. Which
would bend to the other?

17

The next few weeks were exceedingly crucial for the Protestant cause. Young Marie Stuart, by her frailty and apparent helplessness, began to charm the nobles until many of them defected to her side. The majority of these were little concerned with theological issues. Even their previous opposition to the Roman Church had been basically political. They objected to foreign domination, either of the state or of the church.

But now they were free of the French influence, or so they believed, and they were little concerned if Mary, in her private devotions, was Roman Catholic, so long as the Scottish church did not have to pay tribute to Rome.

But if the nobles were charmed by the queen the common people were not. Knox had won for them a spiritual independence which, they believed, was fully as important as the political independence which they had achieved. They had no desire to come under the domination of a foreign spiritual ruler once more. Knox and his preacher colleagues had broken the yoke of ecclesiastical domination and they wanted no restoration of the heavy hand of a foreign pope.

And Knox's preachers were common folk of their own status in life. Furthermore, by action of Parliament the previous year, they had the privilege of electing those who would be their pastors. However the nobles might decide, the common people were with John. They were exceedingly crude in the demonstrations of their loyalty. If Mary appeared in public she might encounter the burning effigy of a priest saying mass or meet some other evidence of their opposition to her reign.

The Edinburgh magistrates aligned themselves with the people and issued a proclamation requiring all "monks, friars, priests, nuns, adulterers, fornicators, and similar filthy persons" to leave town. When the queen visited Stirling a mob drove the priests violently out of the church in her presence.

There were plots and counterplots in both camps, some designed to embarrass John, others the queen. Throughout, John was the only minister at St. Giles, in fact the only minister in Edinburgh, until he was able to engage as his assistant young

John Craig who relieved him of a share of his preaching responsibilities.

Recalling the type of government which John Calvin had established in Geneva and cognizant of the deplorable state of the peasants, John was also engaged in an attempt to build Edinburgh into an ideal city. In addition to his knowledge of the dire poverty of the people two other influences were at work in his mind: Augustine's treatise on *The City of God,* and the Book of Revelation with its delineation of the Kingdom of Heaven.

"The people need more than preaching services," he explained to Craig. "They need food in their stomachs. Our preaching is vain if it does not result in better living conditions for the poor."

"But how can you achieve a betterment of their lot?" John Craig inquired.

"By giving the people a voice in the government," Knox replied.

"Are they ready for such a step?" Craig asked.

"No," John acknowledged. "No people ever are. They must learn by bitter experience how difficult it is to make a government function. They will make many mistakes, but through their errors they will profit and finally they will understand what are the principles by which men are able to live together."

. "Will the queen accept your formula for ruling the city?"

"No. Nor will the nobles," John admitted. "But we must lay the foundations for the future. I am not versed in matters of government as is John Calvin. But it took him many years to establish in Geneva the kind of state which I visualize. And I have come to believe that only in a spiritual and political climate like that of Geneva can the principles of the Reformation be established."

In the summer of 1562 a Jesuit priest, with the approval of the queen, came to Scotland with a commission from the pope to restore the mass. Knox hurried out into the country districts to alert his friends, and in Ayrshire on September fourth Glencairn and seventy-seven leaders of the district signed another "band," promising to resist all efforts of that nature.

In November of the same year word came to John of a program of feasting and revelry in the palace. It appeared as if the queen and her courtiers felt completely assured of the triumph of their cause.

John returned to Edinburgh and on December eighteenth he preached another sermon denunciatory of the queen and her

court. He chose as his text the ominous words, "Understand, O
ye kings, and be warned, ye that judge the earth," and he de-
cried the revelry which had gone on in the palace, likening the
court to that of Nero where, he said, there was "fiddling and
flinging" while Rome burned.

Again the queen summoned him to give an account of himself.
Knox dutifully repaired to the palace to encounter there not
only the queen but a considerable company of courtiers.

"I have been summoned, your majesty, to give account of the
sermon which I preached on last Sabbath. May I ask your grace
who it was among this company who has again charged me with
treason? In order to do so he or they must needs have attended
divine service last Sunday in St. Giles. May I ask your grace
which of your courtiers was present? I do not seem to recall
seeing any one of them in the service."

He hesitated dramatically, awaiting her reply. When none was
volunteered his eyes roved over the assemblage.

"Were you there, Maitland?" he then inquired innocently. "At
one time there was no one more faithful than you, but I do
not recall your being in church for many months past."

Maitland's face turned red but he did not answer.

"What? You were not present? Well, then, who was?"

He reached into his pocket and brought forth the summons
which he read. When he finished he folded it up and again
surveyed the group.

"It seemeth that I am charged with having spoken irreverently
of your majesty in such a manner that I made you appear odious
and contemptible, according to this paper. Surely, someone who
was present made this charge. Else would they have had no
basis, except vile rumor, for thus arraigning me."

Again he paused.

He shook his head and then continued.

"Madam," he said, "this is what frequently happens when one
is unwilling to hear God speak to the comfort of the penitent
and the condemnation of the wicked. If you had been present
in the service yourself in what is, in truth, the national church
of Scotland, you would not have given heed to the false report
of others. Your majesty has now governed us for several years
and yet you have never, to my knowledge, passed through the
portals of the greatest church in your kingdom.

"I have no doubt that proud Herod heard that on one occasion our Master referred to him as 'the fox,' but those who

brought him this report failed to tell how odious it was before God to murder innocent John the Baptist merely as a reward for the dancing of the daughter of a harlot.

"Madam, if those who reported my words had been honest men they would have given you an account of what I said and the circumstances and setting in which the words were uttered.

"Since no one is here who is bold enough to accuse me I can give you, from memory, the substance of my remarks. Firstly, in my sermon I extolled the high office of the crown. Surely that is not treason. I explained that it was a place of dignity and honor to which God called men. I did add, your majesty, that it was most unfortunate that many princes abuse the authority which has been conferred upon them. While murderers and malefactors are welcomed to their courts the saints of God are traduced and banished therefrom. Yet princes ought to be versed in God's law and able to judge between the righteous and unrighteous. But they despise the law of God. In roistering and revelry, instead, do they take delight.

"Now concerning the matter of dancing, I did note that, although in the Scriptures I found nothing said in praise of the practice, I did not utterly condemn it. I did remark that I thought it inadvisable to neglect one's principal vocation in order to engage continually in the performance of it for, surely, it should merely be an exercise and not the purpose for which anyone was created. And I added that dancers ought not to disport themselves, as did the Philistines, for the pleasure to be found in arousing the displeasure of God's people. Is anyone here present who will aver that I said more than that, or that I have left out any relevant statement? If so, with the permission of your grace, I should like to have such an one confront me."

The queen looked about her but no one made bold to answer.

"If there are no charges against me do I have your grace's permission to retire?" he inquired courteously.

She nodded her head. The man had thwarted her again.

As he bowed his way out he heard some of his enemies remark that he looked too sure of himself. He stopped and addressed himself to them.

"Why should the pleasing face of a gentlewoman affright me?" he asked. "I have looked into the faces of many angry men and been unafraid."

Those who had whispered to one another turned away. No one wanted to challenge him.

In the three years since Mary ascended the throne it became more and more evident that the two strong forces in Scotland during that period had become Mary and John Knox. Mary's power lay not in her personality but in the fact that she was queen. Knox's power resided in his preaching. To these two poles gravitated the various parties of the kingdom. Mary had on her side many of the nobles — some of them Protestant in their sympathies — and Knox the common people.

It was unfortunate for Mary that she had been so young when she ascended the throne. She had had an unhappy marriage in her childhood; yet she should have been ripe for a felicitous union. Then, too, her beauty and trusting disposition were her undoing. She engaged in various unfortunate love affairs. These climaxed in marriage to Lord Henry Darnley. This marriage proved unsatisfactory, and her favorite became James Hepburn, the Earl of Bothwell. The people might have accepted her love affairs as prerogatives of royalty were it not for the fact that Knox inveighed against them. In a sense the preacher became the conscience of Scotland.

Again and again, because of these sermons condemnatory of the queen, John would be summoned to the palace for conferences with her. The issue between them was constantly joined. She was the advocate of the principle that royalty could do no wrong: Knox insisted that the queen, as the one appointed by God to rule Scotland, had a responsibility to lead an exemplary life. As the one to whom an abundance of talents had been given it was expected that she would use them for the glory of God.

This concept of the responsibilities of royalty was not commonly accepted at that time. In fact, it was not until the end of the nineteenth century that people began to expect that their monarchs would lead lives of rectitude and probity. To her courtiers Mary was a spoiled darling to be used, if possible, for their own advantage. Her marital experience was unhappy. Lord Darnley was a fop. Her intrigues with the Earl of Bothwell became notorious.

Throughout all of her escapades she turned to Knox as to an inner conscience — but a conscience which she had no intention of heeding — seeking to bend him to her will but realizing throughout that this was impossible. Her frequent summons to him to attend upon her were well-nigh a form of self-punishment. She apparently hoped that he would condone her sins, but she was well aware that he would not.

However, at long last the queen had John cornered. It happened while she was absent from the palace on a visit to western Scotland. She was accompanied by her chaplain who regularly conducted mass for her. The people had come to accept this and, while Knox railed against it, he, too, had recognized the fact that nothing could be done about it. It was the single exception to the law of the realm which he was willing to accept.

During her absence from the palace a priest, other than her own chaplain, celebrated mass, apparently with her approval, in the palace chapel. One Sunday in September, while the Laird of Pitarrow who was Privy Purse in the government, was attending the service at St. Giles a lackey came to him during John's sermon and whispered to him the information that a crowd had forced its way into the palace chapel, and the attendant priest was in danger of his life.

Two of the burgesses of Edinburgh were present at the chapel when this occurred, and they were summoned to appear for trial on October twenty-fourth. Their summons arrived sufficiently in advance of the trial to permit John Knox to lay plans for the event. By this time he had come to the decision that revolution was the only solution for Scotland's trouble. It was time to take a strong stand.

Therefore he sent letters to supporters the length and breadth of Scotland, inviting them to come to Edinburgh to consult with him regarding measures which could be taken in defense of the burgesses. John did not indicate in his letters that he condoned their offense. They had legal authority to stop the mass although they did not exercise it; but there was no excuse for permitting the brawling crowd to enter the chapel.

These letters were sent out on October eighth. Some copies fell into the queen's hands. She decided not to prosecute the charges against the burgesses but instead to bring Knox to trial for high treason.

It seemed a propitious time for such action. The Council of Trent was just closing its meetings which had continued for eighteen years. While no conclusion in the matter had been reached Mary was aware that the last item for discussion was a plan to excommunicate Elizabeth. If this were done Mary could lay claim to the English throne. She received assurances from Spain that a Spanish fleet would attack England if Elizabeth were to be disciplined thus by the church. The prospect for Mary's accession to the English crown seemed bright. If she could eliminate John Knox one obstacle to her accession would be overcome. Thus she charged him with high treason and set the trial date a few days before Christmas, 1563.

Lord James Stuart and Maitland, fearful of the results of such a trial, went to the queen to plead with her to stop it, but to no avail. They then visited Knox to urge him to make his peace with Mary.

Both of these men had aided John during the time that the queen regent had occupied the throne but they, although Protestant in their sympathies, had made their peace with the young monarch and were high in her counsels. Since they were politicians first and Protestants secondarily they were eager to continue the status quo.

"You were wrong, Messer Knox, to summon such a conference," Maitland remarked. "Admit your error and make peace with her majesty."

"Wherein did I wrong?" Knox mildly inquired.

"Your letters smacked of high treason," Lord James replied.

"Since when has it become treason to urge the support of officers who are seeking to obey the laws of Scotland?" Knox countered.

"Even you must admit that the burgesses went too far in permitting the brawling in the palace chapel," Maitland retorted.

"It was most unfortunate," John admitted, "but the priest was violating the law of the land in celebrating the mass."

"But it has now been celebrated for several years in that same place," Stuart reminded him. "We do not approve it but it has been tacitly agreed that the queen's religion is a private matter."

"Aye, we have winked at her evasion of the law," John agreed, "but this is different. The queen and her chaplain were elsewhere. This was one mass too many. It was the entering wedge of the celebration of this heathen rite everywhere in the realm. Those burgesses did not act with my approval. Nor did they consult with me regarding their proposed stand. But since they took it I shall stand back of them and arouse all of Scotland in their defense."

"That is your final word?" asked Maitland.

"That is my last word," replied Knox.

Stuart and Maitland then consulted with other Protestant leaders, among them an attorney, John Spens. Spens was a sturdy Protestant and friend of Knox. He felt that John had quite evidently exceeded himself and gone so far that the charge of treason could be proved.

Hence he, too, paid a visit to the reformer.

"You know where my sympathies lie," he remarked. "I have been on your side ever since you first declared yourself. But I tell you, Messer Knox, that you have placed yourself in a position where your conviction on the charge of treason is almost inevitable. Lord James and Maitland believe that you can make peace with the queen if you will only admit that you have gone too far. Let them represent you before her majesty and I will go with them to plead your cause."

"But wherein does my cause need pleading?" John asked. "I merely called some men together for a meeting. At what time did that become a crime in Scotland?"

"Only when such a meeting is held for the purpose of defying the queen."

"Such defiance is not intended," Knox said. "We have merely urged Protestants to attend the trial of the burgesses to see that justice is done."

"But the letter which you dispatched to your friends . . ."

"What of it?"

"It urged them to come to Edinburgh to plan for ways by which Mary might be overthrown."

"Have you seen a copy of the letter?"

"I have not."

"Well, then, let me read it to you."

Thereupon John took from his desk a copy of the letter and began to read it aloud. It had been merely a call to his friends to come to Edinburgh to consider ways and means to defend the accused burgesses and a plea that they should remain for the ensuing trial.

"That is all that you wrote?" Spens inquired.

"That is all."

"You did not append additional paragraphs in the letters to your very close friends?"

"No. The letters were identical."

"Well, then, I cannot see that they contain anything treasonable. Always a subject has the right to address or appeal to a monarch. Nor is there anything in our law forbidding assembly. And, since trials are public spectacles, a defendant or his friends may encourage attendance of his partisans in order to afford a proper balance in his favor. You are certain that you went no further? You did not condemn her majesty for bringing these men to trial?"

"I did not."

Spens meditated for a short time.

"May I suggest, Messer Knox, that you engage counsel for this trial. Since you have been notified so long in advance of the occasion I presume that the queen is marshaling her most eminent lawyers to prosecute you. True," he remarked with a smile, "you have never come off second best in your previous encounters with her majesty but I am certain that she and the prosecutors will leave no stone unturned to prove you guilty of high treason. I would gladly undertake to defend you if you would wish to avail yourself of my services."

"I am indeed grateful, Messer Spens," John replied, "but are you aware of the danger that you face? If you defend me you will be branded as my friend and yourself may be subject to the penalties which the court — which is her majesty — may see fit to impose upon me. I strongly suspect that they will hope to mete out to me the death penalty."

"They can scarce go that far," Spens replied, "but I have no fear of reprisal if they have that in mind. Of a truth, I would not defend you if I thought that in any way you had been treasonable to the crown but I cannot see that you have done aught amiss."

A few days before Christmas, at between six and seven o'clock in the evening John Knox presented himself in the palace at Holyrood to stand trial for the crime of high treason.

The queen was in holiday mood, gaily attired and surrounded by her courtiers. She had never been more beautiful. She wore a crown and jewels, apparently for the purpose of impressing both John Knox and her entourage. She was seated on her throne which was on a raised dais at one end of the great hall. Knox had to traverse the length of the hall in order to approach her throne.

In contrast to the brilliant plumage of the courtiers, Knox's simple attire made him appear like a sparrow in the midst of a flock of peacocks. Mary's eyes had noted him as soon as he entered but she paid no attention to him. He was accompanied by Sir Douglas Mackenzie and John Spens.

The courtiers and counselors turned to look at John, staring at him distastefully.

Finally Mary deigned to notice him. She began to laugh. Some of the courtiers joined in her mirth although they did not know the cause of it.

Mary turned to the courtiers nearest her.

"Do you know why I laugh?" she inquired.

They shook their heads.

She pointed a dainty finger at Knox.

"That man once made me weep," she said, "and never shed a tear himself. I will see now if I can make him sorrow."

Although Maitland and James Stuart had been to call upon him, the former now appeared in the guise of prosecutor. He arose in his place and declaimed, "Her majesty is informed that ye have conspired to arouse her subjects against her. She has in her hand a copy of a letter which you wrote to various of her subjects, to which is appended your signature."

The queen handed Maitland one of the copies which she had obtained.

"Ask him if that is his signature," she commanded.

Maitland handed the letter to Knox who glanced at it and then said, "It is my signature. Nor do I need to read the letter, for I know its contents. Of a truth, I had so much confidence in my scribe that I signed blank sheets of paper and let him copy out the text of the letter above my signature."

"That is more confidence than I would have shown," Maitland suggested grimly.

"When one has faith in his fellows he is not suspicious," Knox retorted with a smile.

"Read your own letter," the queen demanded pettishly. "Then you shall answer to the charges which are brought against you."

Knox read in a loud, clear voice. Everyone paid the strictest attention. The letter was short and was soon finished.

When John had completed the reading the queen looked about her and then demanded, "My lords, have you ever heard a more despiteful and treasonable letter?"

No one replied to her query.

Maitland rose in his place at the table.

"Now that you have had time to consider the matter, Messer Knox, are you not truly sorry that you penned this epistle? Doubtless, in the heat of passion and your zeal to defend the burgesses, you could pen such a letter without thinking too much on its implications but, as you have had time to consider it, do you not sincerely repent of having caused offense to her majesty?" inquired Maitland, assuming his most placating tone.

"Offense?" returned John innocently. "Would you be so kind as to tell me in what way I have offended her majesty? I cannot express contrition for an act which had no intent of causing anyone offense."

"If you had done nothing more than convoke subjects of the crown that were offense enough."

"Oh, surely not, my Lord Secretary," John replied, relishing the opportunity to debate with Maitland, particularly in view of the fact that the poor man was not certain of his ground. "Remember that there is much difference between a lawful assembly and an unlawful one. If any assembly is per se unlawful then every religious service held in Scotland, whether by priests of the Roman Church or by Reformation advocates, is unlawful and all ministers and priests violate the law. Furthermore, whenever three or four people meet together in a home or tavern they break the law. If it is unlawful for such assemblies then I freely confess that I have broken the law for I have conducted many services and I have met with many groups of persons. But is there one here who has not violated such a law? And, prior to this day, no one accused me of a crime in merely assembling people for meetings or services."

"But times are different," Maitland argued.

"My lord," John replied, "I can see no difference between then and now save that in former times Satan went about unmasked but now he wears a light disguise. Formerly he was prone to open tyranny toward God's elect; now he masks oppression with the cloak of justice. I admit that I am aware of that difference but . . ."

"Enough of this," remarked the queen curtly, interrupting his discourse.

Looking down the table she inquired, "My lords, have we not heard enough? He admits that he convoked my subjects without my authority. Is not that treason? What more do we need than this confession before we pass sentence upon him?"

Ruthven stood in his place, looked defiantly at the queen.

" 'Tis not as simple as that, your majesty," he said. "Every day John Knox convokes your subjects for prayer and a sermon. More than a mere act of convocation must needs be proved if this assembly is to condemn him."

Ruthven was doubtless on the queen's side. But he was aware of the danger of passing sentence on Knox for the simple act of convocation. If Knox could be condemned for so doing then the precedent, once established, could be cited for other such meetings. Three or four men invited to a man's house — no matter for what reason — could become an unlawful convocation and, should he be out of favor with the queen, the excuse for his arrest and imprisonment. An adverse decision against Knox could become a decision which would affect every subject in Mary's realm.

"Hold your tongue," Mary commanded him curtly. "Messer Knox does not need you to defend him. He can speak for himself."

"Thank you, your grace," Knox replied with a courtly bow. "I opened my defense on the premise that not all convocations of your Majesty's subjects are unlawful. Were it otherwise three or four shepherds in the highlands could not gather about a common camp-fire; five or six housewives could not meet in the market-place and complain about the cost of mutton. Lord Ruthven has indicated that he agrees with that premise in substance."

The queen held up her hand to stay him.

"I have nothing against your convening my subjects to hear your sermons," she said. "I have naught against your religion. But by what authority do you call my subjects together for other meetings without my permission?"

"Gladly will I answer that question, your majesty," he said, "for in all of the years that I have spent in Scotland since I left the priesthood I have never convened so many as four persons by mine own authority. When I have preached or spoken to any company of people it has been by the authority of the kirk which, as your majesty is well aware, although you yourself adhere to a foreign church, is the only true kirk in your realm.

"If your grace complains that this was done without your permission, I must remind you in all sincerity that everything which God has blessed since you came to the throne has been without your permission. And may I further remind your majesty that, by your permission and with your authority, soldiers of the crown have woefully persecuted followers of the true kirk. What I have done has been accomplished with the authority of that true kirk, according to the laws of the realm. I cannot see, therefore, that I have done anything wrong."

Passionately the queen made reply, addressing the nobles, "He has condemned himself out of his own mouth. Ye have just heard him accuse his monarch of cruelty. I believe there are acts of Parliament to deal with such an offense."

Some of the courtiers nodded their heads vigorously to indicate their approval: The queen's counselors maintained a stony calm.

The queen then played her trump card. She turned to a section of the letter in which John had suggested that the burgesses were being brought to trial to prepare the way for the queen to execute cruelty upon a greater number of people.

"What do you say to that?" she asked sarcastically.

"Is it lawful for me to answer this charge myself, madam, or shall I be damned without a hearing?" John inquired courteously, but with an overtone of skepticism in his voice.

"Answer if you will," she retorted. "I doubt if you can squirm out of that one."

"Well, then, I would first like to know, madam, if your majesty is unaware of the plan of the obstinate papists to exterminate all Protestants, and do away with the true doctrine which by them is proclaimed in this realm?"

The queen made no reply.

However, one of her counselors spoke up.

"God forbid that the lives of the faithful should be placed in jeopardy," he exclaimed, "or that the papists should determine what doctrine shall be preached in Scotland!"

John realized that some members of the council, at least, understood the issue. It made little difference what happened to him. The important thing was that Scotland should be forever free of papal domination. If that could be assured he would gladly burn for it.

His plea, therefore, was basically for Scotland.

"I am confident that my lords will all grant that it was a barbarity to condemn to death the multitude who have professed the Gospel of Christ," he argued. "If this were done only once or twice it might be assumed that it had been done through no intent but, instead, through inadvertence. But it has often been attempted through the use of force. Yet Providence has disappointed them and, in consequence, they invented more crafty and dangerous practices still. That is, they have sought to make the queen a party under color of law; and what they could not accomplish by open force they have sought to perform by crafty deceit.

"Who of you, my lords, assume that the insatiable cruelty of the papists — within this realm, I mean — shall end in the murdering of the two brethren who have been unjustly summoned to trial and more unjustly accused? Read through the acts of Parliament if you will, madam, and you will discover that I have not in any way broken them. I did not accuse you of cruelty in my letter, your grace. But I do say, without fear of contradiction, that the pestilent papists have inflamed your majesty against two loyal burgesses. I will add further that those who thus kindled your anger against them are the sons of the devil and must, therefore, obey the desires of their father who has been a liar and a man-slayer from the beginning."

John was just proceeding to warm up to the task of defending the burgesses. He had apparently forgotten that he was on trial himself. His tones were orotund. His eyes sparked fire.

At this point Maitland interrupted him.

"You forget where you stand, Messer Knox," he said with a smile. "You are not now in the pulpit."

A laugh greeted this sally in which John also joined.

Knox now addressed himself to the queen.

"Your majesty," he said, "I know that you are of a meek, gentle and kindly nature. If you would surround yourself with counselors of like spirit you could have a great reign in this land. But a gentle person like yourself could be corrupted by evil counsel. And I say to you now that the papists who presently have your ear are dangerous counselors, and such your gracious mother found them to be."

"Hear! Hear!" shouted many of the counselors.

Others, among them the queen's chaplain, glared at Knox.

Thereupon the vote was taken. Only those who were seated at the table were entitled to vote. By an overwhelming majority John Knox was adjudged innocent of the crime of high treason.

The queen burst into tears.

John Knox arose in his place.

"I thank you, me Lords," he said, "for this vindication. And I would again assert my loyalty to the crown of Scotland and the gracious monarch who now occupies the throne. I have lived in other lands but my heart has always been in Scotland, wherever I have been.

"But I have longed for a Scotland free of foreign dominion.

I have longed for a Scotland free of all ties to France. I love France. It is a great and beautiful country, a land which is also struggling for freedom. But I would not want Scotland to be under the domination of France.

"And, by the same token, I would have our native land free also of the dominion of a foreign pope. I grew up in the church of which he is the head. I love that church for what it was and what it may become, but I would not bow my knee to that church again.

"Instead, I would bow the knee only to my Lord and Saviour, Jesus Christ, and, as a loyal Scot, to my monarch.

"There are thousands of us in Scotland, madam, who feel as I do. We have bought our liberties with the blood of martyrs. I have paid for mine with this back which bent over the oars in a French galley. During the years when we were, in effect, subjects of France we yearned for the time when we would have a monarch for our country alone — but a sovereign who, like us, would be Protestant.

"You could have a great reign, madam — the greatest. Could you but cease your intrigues and bend your efforts to rule this land wisely, courageously, with kindness and firmness, all Scots would rally to support you. That is what the vast majority of your subjects yearn for. They pray earnestly and with fervor that you may be a wise queen and that you may have a long and happy reign."

The queen made no answer. She arose and her counselors with her. All stood respectfully as she made her way majestically from the great hall. John's eyes, as well as those of the counselors, followed her.

After she had departed John turned to Maitland.

"Could you arrange for a private audience with her majesty?" he asked the counselor. "The queen was in tears for a part of the time. That is a good sign. Her conscience troubles her."

Maitland smiled grimly.

"For all of your experience with the sex, Messer John," he said, "you evidence a surprising lack of knowledge of womankind. 'Twas not her conscience that brought on the tears. They were occasioned by the fact that she was woefully thwarted. She wanted your head on a pike at the city gates."

"Nay, my friend," Knox replied. "I believe that she is close to a decision for the right."

Maitland shrugged his shoulders.

"It can be arranged," he said, "but I believe it will avail nothing."

"If the conference would be just between the two of us and her majesty," John suggested tentatively. "If we could speak to her when those who whisper in her ear are absent . . ."

"It can be done," Maitland agreed.

18

Two weeks later the summons came in the form of a personal letter from Maitland. He wrote:

> Her majesty will grant us an audience three days hence. I have conversed with her and have assured her that you have naught in mind for the meeting but her personal welfare and the good of Scotland. But remember that she is a prideful creature. Treat her with tact and deference. Much good may come of the meeting.
>
> Above all, friend John, do not act as if you were in the pulpit. She is afraid of your preaching. Therefore, be the kind man that you are, understanding, human.

John pondered the letter. Again he wondered just where Maitland stood. At times he seemed to be on the side of the Reformation. At other times he apparently allied himself to the enemies of reform. Yet what he wrote about the queen was probably true. Doubtless her majesty was afraid of him. And Maitland was possibly right about his preaching. He would have to refrain from indulging in his penchant for delivering a sermon. *If only he could counsel with her majesty as he had so often counseled women of lesser station in the past. And if she would only listen.*

He was prepared to compromise with her — although not in essential matters. He knew that the ideal way in which to bring about a reformation was by degrees. To change long ingrained habits of worship overnight was well-nigh impossible. But how could reformation be accomplished gradually?

How gradual could one be in ridding Scotland of the emissaries of the pope? If you gave them a year in which to close their work would not that time be spent in indoctrinating their congregations so that when they left their congregations would be more intransigent than ever in their resistance to reform. Yet John made up his mind that he would be patient with the queen, kind and long-suffering. He would let her see that he had in his heart only a sincere desire that she might have a reign in Scotland which would enshrine her forever in the hearts of her people.

However, there was another factor which disturbed John. The gossip which had come to him from the palace regarding her love affairs was disquieting. Could one who was so concerned with personal romance and who was apparently so promiscuous in her affairs learn to govern wisely? If only she could surround herself with advisers who could not only counsel with her concerning affairs of state but affairs of the heart as well!

Maitland greeted John when he entered the palace.

"Her majesty is awaiting us," Maitland informed him, "and there will be no others present. I feel certain that the audience will result in good for the cause."

Maitland conducted John to a small room off the great hall. A fire was burning on a tiny hearth located in a corner of the simply furnished room. The queen was already present, attired simply in a flowing gown, and was seated on an ordinary chair. Without the trappings of royalty she seemed a simple young woman, slightly built, with good, regular features.

From the grim look on her face John assumed that she would be stiff and unyielding, but he realized that this was due in part to the fact that she evidently feared the meeting. She inclined her head slightly but did not speak when he entered.

Maitland broke the silence.

"At your majesty's gracious command, John Knox has come hither for the conference," he said.

"It was kind of your majesty to arrange for this meeting," John vouchsafed quietly. "I hope that much good may result for Scotland."

"I hope so, too," she agreed politely, but added with a flash of fire, "yet I would warn you, Messer Knox, that your preaching will not sway me. I am a Catholic and such I will remain to the end of my days."

"But I, too, am Catholic, your majesty," John replied, "and I will remain such forever. I am not one of those who would destroy the Christian faith, but I belong to the Church. The difference between us is that I have forsworn my allegiance to

Rome. Yet I am a minister in the true catholic and universal church, the only head of which is the Lord Jesus Christ Himself."

"I have been taught to believe that there is one church only and the head of that Church is the pope," she asserted. "And his is the sole authority to represent the Saviour on earth."

"Come, your majesty," said Maitland heartily. "I did not bring Messer Knox to argue with your grace upon matters of theology or churchmanship, but rather to see if the two of you may not find some common ground upon which you can meet for the good of Scotland."

"He made me promise before I came that I would not preach," Knox assured her with a smile.

"What, then, is the purpose of our meeting?" the young queen asked coldly.

"It occurred to us that there might be some way in which John Knox might advise your majesty concerning the affairs of the kirk," Maitland explained. "'Twould be helpful to your majesty if you had someone in government who was versed in such matters, and no one is more representative of the kirk than he. I might add that his advice would be especially valuable in your majesty's relations with England. He was chaplain to Edward VI while he lived in England and he hath many friends who are highly placed in government there."

Mary's eyes narrowed. "There are those in Scotland who insist that I am the rightful occupant of that throne," she remarked.

"For the good of Scotland and for your majesty's own welfare I trust that you will not listen to them," John intervened. "If you were to strive to occupy that throne it would only end in disaster for you and your kingdom."

Mary bridled at once.

"My advisers inform me that my claim to the throne is much stronger than Elizabeth's," she insisted.

"But she is occupying it," Maitland reminded her.

"England would welcome the true monarch with open arms," Mary said.

"That is not something with which I would concern myself," John interposed, "but I would be fearful of the results if you should seek to win that throne. I am concerned for your majesty's welfare when I proffer this word of counsel."

"My true friends advise me differently," she said curtly.

"Your truest friends are not those you have imported from France, not the hangers-on of the court, the nobles who oppress the people, who fought against them at Perth and Stirling," exclaimed John, working up to a peroration.

Maitland coughed discreetly. "Nay, nay, Messer Knox," he said. "We were to have no sermons today, you will remember."

"My apologies, your majesty," John murmured in contrition. "I trust you will forgive my zeal, but it is as much in behalf of your majesty's welfare as it is for the good of Scotland."

Mary's face flushed. "You have indicated quite clearly, I think, how far apart we are in our thinking," she said coldly. "You have no interest in me or my welfare. Your sole concern is for a kirk made up of heretics."

"So the *paip* regardeth us, I know," John said, "but we are not heretics in the sight of God. We stand with The Eternal against the pope."

Maitland intervened at this point.

"I should add, your majesty," he remarked judiciously, "that, although he uses strong language, when John Knox speaks he does not only for himself but for the vast majority of your subjects for they believe as he does. And I know that your majesty is concerned to know what your people are thinking."

"I could not care less," Mary replied coldly. "Is Scotland more important than the throne, the common rabble than she who, by the grace of God, occupies the throne?"

"I dare to say that Scotland is," Knox retorted boldly. "No monarch is greater than the people over whom he rules. There is not even any need for a monarch save as he hath subjects, and, while the monarch reigns, he does so for the good of the people."

"But people were created to serve monarchs," Mary replied.

"Nay, your majesty, from the beginning of time governments were erected to serve the governed. A monarch is, in effect, the servant of those over whom he — or she — reigns," John ventured.

"A strange theory, indeed!" responded Mary.

"Perhaps one should say instead that they were created for mutual service," Maitland remarked judiciously.

"Nor can I accept that," Mary said icily.

"No, I suspect that you cannot," Maitland agreed with a sigh, "but that is the spirit of the Scots. They are a bold people. By comparison with the French among whom you were raised they would seem to be crude indeed. But they are also warm-hearted and, if they love their monarch, would lay down their lives on their monarch's behalf. But you must win their love if you would win their loyalty."

"I care for neither."

"But your majesty needs both," Maitland replied. "That is what Lord James Stuart and I have sought to explain to you. And John Knox is typical of the entire commonalty. In a true sense he speaks for your people."

"I like not his voice," said Mary.

"Mayhap not, your majesty," John interrupted, "but far better my cracked voice than the strident tones of a mob. I knew nothing of the invasion of the palace chapel when it occurred, and I do not condone the event, but it was the voice of the people of Scotland speaking — in harsh tones, to be sure, but speaking nonetheless. We do not want it to occur again but it may unless your majesty takes steps to avoid it."

"You threaten me?"

"Nay. I warn you — and the warning is that of a friend."

"No friend would speak to me in that fashion."

"A friend would, your majesty, who is concerned for your welfare and that of your realm," Maitland suggested courteously.

"The audience is over," Mary announced curtly. "It is evident that Messer Knox has no intention of bending his knee to his queen but intends to continue harassing his lawful monarch. Well, so be it. Our discussion is fruitless. Messer Knox, you are dismissed."

She clapped her hands and two armed guards appeared at the door.

"Show Messer Knox to the gates," she commanded.

John rose to leave.

"Again I am sorry, your majesty," John remarked, "if I have done aught to offend you. Such was not my intention. Instead, I would that heaven should smile upon your reign that it may be long and prosperous, and that it shall be one which will long be remembered in Scotland.

"But I fear, your majesty, that it is fated otherwise. You are the innocent victim of intrigues which go on in the palace, but you will pay for those intrigues — possibly with your life. If you will not listen to your Protestant counselors you will lose the support of your Protestant subjects who far outnumber those who profess allegiance to Rome.

"If you essay an adventure in England at the advice and counsel of your fawning courtiers, you may forfeit your life. Your

Scots would not support you in an attempt to win the English crown. That is utter folly. But if you will not heed these words which I am confident your wiser counselors would also give you then the results of your adventure will be upon your own head."

Mary held up her hand imperiously.

"These are the ravings of a madman," she exclaimed. "Go and never return to the palace. I do not want to see your face again."

"As you will, madam," Knox replied. "Only remember that neither you nor Scotland had a warmer friend than John Knox. If I have opposed you it has been because of my sincere love for this land. But I would have Scotland a nation of free men. Scots must breathe the air of liberty or they die. Scotland must be free or it will perish as a nation. God save Scotland!"

Head held as high as his bent back would allow, John left the room, a guard on either side. He could do nothing more to save the queen. He hoped that he had saved Scotland, but the destinies of the rugged land of his birth were in the keeping of The Eternal.